PRAISE FOR JESSICA DAY GEORGE'S

Tuesdays at the *Castle* series

"These kids are clever, as is George's lively adventure. May pique castle envy." —*Kirkus Reviews* on *Tuesdays at the Castle*

"This story puts an unexpected spin on the typical princess tale. Readers will root equally for crafty Celie and for her castle." —*Library Media Connection* on *Tuesdays at the Castle*

"There is a warmth here that is utterly irresistible." —BCCB on *Tuesdays at the Castle*

"A charming, adventurous story with a spirit that will appeal to fans of Kate DiCamillo's *The Tale of Despereaux*. . . . *Tuesdays at the Castle* is all the more enjoyable for the intelligent, strong characters who dwell within its pages and castle walls." —Shelf Awareness on *Tuesdays at the Castle*

"There is plenty to charm readers in this second book in the series. . . . The Castle is a character in its own right, and readers will be fascinated to learn more about its history." —*School Library Journal* on *New York Times* bestselling *Wednesdays in the Tower*

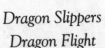

FRIDAYS
with the *Wizards*

JESSICA DAY GEORGE

BLOOMSBURY
NEW YORK LONDON OXFORD NEW DELHI SYDNEY

First published in the United States of America in February 2016
by Bloomsbury Children's Books
Paperback edition published in February 2017
www.bloomsbury.com

Bloomsbury is a registered trademark of Bloomsbury Publishing Plc

For information about permission to reproduce selections from this book, write to
Permissions, Bloomsbury Children's Books, 1385 Broadway, New York, New York 10018
Bloomsbury books may be purchased for business or promotional use. For information on
bulk purchases please contact Macmillan Corporate and Premium Sales Department at
specialmarkets@macmillan.com

The Library of Congress has cataloged the hardcover edition as follows:
George, Jessica Day.
Fridays with the wizards / by Jessica Day George.
pages   cm.
Sequel to: Thursdays with the crown.
Summary: When the dangerous ancient wizard Arkwright escapes the dungeon and goes
missing within the Castle, Princess Celie must find the wizard and save her family.
ISBN 978-1-61963-429-9 (hardcover) • ISBN 978-1-61963-430-5 (e-book)
[1. Fairy tales. 2. Castles—Fiction. 3. Princesses—Fiction.
4. Brothers and sisters—Fiction. 5. Wizards—Fiction.] I. Title.
PZ8.G3295Fr 2016   [Fic]—dc23   2015008529

ISBN 978-1-68119-204-8 (paperback)

Book design by Donna Mark
Typeset by Newgen Knowledge Works (P) Ltd, Chennai, India
Printed and bound in the U.S.A. by Berryville Graphics Inc., Berryville, Virginia
4 6 8 10 9 7 5 3

All papers used by Bloomsbury Publishing, Inc., are natural, recyclable products
made from wood grown in well-managed forests. The manufacturing processes
conform to the environmental regulations of the country of origin.

*Lovingly dedicated to my boys—now
leave your sister alone!*

Chapter
1

It was good to be home.

Celie had spent her entire life in Castle Glower, and she wasn't sorry about it. She especially wasn't sorry now that she'd been to another world and been filthy and hungry and cold and scared. No one ever went cold or hungry inside the Castle, and now with her entire family around her and no one threatening them or the Castle, Celie had no reason to be scared.

The Castle loved Celie, Celie loved the Castle, and she was in no hurry to leave it again.

Her sister, Lilah, on the other hand, was of a very different opinion.

"I'm so bored, I might be dying," Lilah announced. "I can't believe that Father won't even let us go to Sleyne City!"

"With a *griffin*? How are you going to take Juliet all the way to the city?" Celie was lying on her back on the window seat in Lilah's rooms, idly throwing a ball for her own griffin, Rufus, while Lilah groomed her smaller griffin, Juliet.

"Why not?" Lilah brushed vigorously at Juliet's golden-furred hindquarters, which were gleaming like real gold, she had been groomed so thoroughly. "Shouldn't the people of Sleyne City get to see the griffins?"

"Half of the city has already come here," Celie said, feeling a bit grumpy now that Lilah had reminded her. Rufus pressed his ball, now dripping with drool, into her hand and she threw it quickly, shaking her hand dry.

What she'd said was true: the halls of the Castle had been filled with a continuous stream of petitioners making up any reason they could to gain an audience with Celie's father, King Glower. All they really wanted was to catch a glimpse of the two dozen griffins that Celie, Lilah, their brother Rolf, and their friends Pogue and Lulath had brought back from another world. It was easy to oblige them: most of the griffins liked to sun themselves on the top of the Castle's outer wall, and, much to the excitement of the Glower family and the court, the formidable griffin king had adopted the human king.

Lord Griffin, as Celie had dubbed him, sat beside her father's throne while King Glower heard petitions and stared with yellow-eyed intensity at the petitioners, who usually forgot what they'd come to ask and stumbled out after a few muttered words. No one minded. As King Glower explained, how could they expect any different? There had been griffins on the flag of Castle Glower since the Castle had first appeared in Sleyne, but no one had known that the creatures were real until just a few weeks ago.

"But they can't all come here," Lilah said reasonably. "We should go to them! And we should go to Grath—it's only fair!"

"How is that fair? Or unfair if we don't go to Grath?" Celie asked in confusion.

"Well, Lulath's been here for a year," Lilah pointed out. "And we've never reciprocated by sending someone to their court to visit. It's like we're keeping him hostage!" She flourished the brush.

"He came for Mummy and Daddy's *funeral*," Celie reminded her, "only they weren't dead. And no one is making him stay."

"Celie!" Lilah looked up at her in shock.

Celie put one hand to her mouth. She hadn't meant that to sound so terrible. She felt horrified, and more than that, disloyal: Prince Lulath of Grath had been a good friend to her, and to her entire family. She loved having him in the Castle and would be very sad when he went home. But Celie still didn't want to leave the Castle.

"I'm sorry," Celie said. "You know I adore Lulath! But . . . if he does leave, he has Lorcan—a griffin of his very own he can show off in Grath and Sleyne City and everywhere else along the way."

3

"I suppose," Lilah said, mollified. She took on a wheedling tone. "But don't you want to go to Grath? You said you did just last week! Don't you remember that?"

Celie did remember that. Just a week ago, she and Lilah had been in the griffins' exercise tower above Celie's bedroom, and Lilah had broached the subject of going to Grath, and then even farther.

Lilah was fascinated by the story of the unicorns that had once lived in Sleyne. They had been either eaten or chased away by the griffins, which had arrived unexpectedly one day generations ago with the Castle. The griffins had been fleeing a plague in the Castle's home world, a plague that had later killed all the griffins and most of their riders. The unicorns, meanwhile, were rumored to have fled to Grath, where they were loaded onto ships that sailed for Larien, the Land of a Thousand Waterfalls. Once there they ascended a rainbow into the sky and were never seen again.

Lilah had wanted a unicorn desperately when she was small, and it seemed that the longing for such a pet had not abated. Not even when she had a griffin to care for. And baby griffins needed a great deal of care.

"There!" Lilah set aside the brush. "Who's the most beautiful girl in the world? Who is she? Is she my girl? Is she?"

Juliet wiggled with pleasure and nipped lovingly at Lilah's fingers.

4

Rufus stopped tearing at his ball and ran over to Celie. She sat up so that she could stroke his head and assure him that he was the handsomest griffin in the world, and that everyone loved him. Rufus had been the only griffin in Sleyne for the first three months of his life, and he sometimes got jealous of the attention the other griffins attracted.

"Could you at least put in a good word with Father and Mother, if Lulath asks me to go to Grath with him?" Lilah pleaded.

"Is Lulath going home?"

Celie felt her heart constrict a little. Would Lulath come back? He was third or possibly even fourth in line to the throne of Grath—surely his family could spare him for a while longer?

"He might be," Lilah said, smiling a secret smile. "But only if I—we—wanted to see Grath."

Celie squinted at her sister. What was Lilah getting at? It sounded like Lulath would only go home if Lilah accompanied him. "Are you saying—"

The door of Lilah's room slammed open, hitting the opposite wall. Their brother Bran, in full, flowing robes and round wizard's hat, burst through. Right on his heels was Pogue Parry, the son of the village blacksmith who had been recently knighted for their adventure in the ancient world of the Castle.

"Are you all right?" Bran yelled.

"What? Yes!" Celie jumped up, dumping Rufus's head off her lap. "What's happening? Where are Mummy and Daddy?"

"They're in the throne room, but— He's not here?" Bran circled the room, looking wild.

"Bran, the stables," Pogue said in a strained voice.

"Yes! You're right!" Bran started to run back out of the room and stopped dead. "Which ones, though? You don't think he'd try the griffins?"

Pogue cursed and he and Bran both ran out of the room, leaving Celie and Lilah staring.

"What's happening?" Lilah called after them, but they didn't stop.

Celie didn't bother to shout; she just raced past Lilah and Juliet, with Rufus at her side. It was easy to follow Bran and Pogue; she could hear their boots on the stones of the corridor to her left, hear them shouting to each other as they ran.

"What's happening?" Lilah called out again, but she was right behind Celie, running down the corridor with Juliet in her arms.

"I've called out the guard," Rolf yelled as they all reached the main hall.

The front doors were open, and there were two guards standing with spears at the ready, waiting for Bran's command. The doors to the throne room were open as well, and Celie could hear their father shouting orders.

6

"I'll go to the griffin stables," Bran said. "You're with me." He pointed to one of the guards. "Pogue, you and Rolf take the horse stables, and him." He pointed to the other guard.

"Bran, what is happening?" Celie did shout now, while Rufus and Juliet flapped their wings and screeched, disturbed by the tension and the raised voices.

"It's Arkwright," Bran said, pausing only briefly on his way out the doors. "He's escaped from the dungeons."

Chapter
2

⟨⟨⟨⟨⟨◦⟩⟩⟩⟩⟩

Arkwright wasn't in the horse stable or either of the griffin stables. The horses and the griffins were all accounted for, and none of the guards or stable hands had seen any sign of the wizard. Which was a problem.

"How did he just disappear?" Bran snarled, throwing his hat down on the seat of his chair in the throne room.

The sun was setting, and the Glower family and the entire staff of the Castle had turned over every bed, chair, and rug looking for Arkwright. The wizard, unfortunately, was nowhere to be found.

"He's a wizard," Rolf said. "Probably made himself invisible and walked right out after breakfast, with no one the wiser."

"He can't," Bran said. "I've made sure of it! I placed spells on every inch of his cell!" He picked up his hat and began to wring it like a dishcloth.

"The Castle didn't notice him leaving," their father said.

King Glower the Seventy-ninth was sitting on his throne and wearing the crown of the first king of the Castle. Celie and the others had brought it back for him along with a ring, both taken from the tomb of the Builder of the Castle. The crown and rings were the tools that the kings of old had used to communicate with the Castle, but they'd been hidden with the Builder when the Castle was brought to Sleyne. Now that Celie's father had them, he was able to feel the Castle and ask it to make changes, instead of having to wait and see what it would do.

King Glower paused and stared into space for a moment. "No," he said. "It didn't notice at all."

"Can't we just say good riddance, and forget he was ever here?" Lilah demanded. "I vote we bar the gates against him and simply get on with our lives!"

"Ah, but our Lilah, it is not being such the easy thing," Lulath said. He was sitting on the floor, uncaring of his richly embroidered velvet tunic and silk breeches, playing with his griffin and his four dogs all at once. Both the clothes and the animals made it hard to take Lulath seriously, but his next words were grim enough to sink in.

"A man of the very great evil, such as Arkwright is being, must being watched at all times, or more evil he is being the author of."

"Lulath's right," Bran said. "Arkwright split the Castle, brought half of it here, pretty much watched everyone and their griffins die, erased the Castle's history, and spent the next few centuries making sure it stayed that way. He belongs in a dungeon under constant watch."

"Or dead," Pogue muttered.

"He hasn't done anything we can execute him for," King Glower reminded them. "Although it would have been easier," he said under his breath.

"Owen!" Queen Celina looked shocked.

Owen was the name the king had been given when he was born, before he became Glower the Seventy-ninth, and only the queen ever used it . . . and only when she was upset. The rest of the time, he was "darling," just like the children. Until she was five, Celie had thought that her father's name was Darling, and that'd she'd been named Celie-Darling, after him.

"At the very least," Rolf said, "we should have sent him back to his precious *Glorious Arkower*." The name dripped with sarcasm.

"That didn't seem to be the right solution, either," King Glower said. He rubbed his forehead, just below the heavy crown.

"No, the Castle didn't like that idea," Celie agreed. "Otherwise it would have just sent him back. He was here for weeks before the Castle sent us, and just us, to Hatheland, or the Glorious Arkower, or whatever you want to call it." She suppressed a shudder at the memory. They'd thought the Castle was shaking itself to bits, and when it all settled, they were in another world. Alone. "He was here for weeks after, as well. We've been to Hatheland twice now," she reminded them. "But it's never sent *him* back there."

"Celie's right," her father said. "I think the Castle knows how much trouble that man could cause if he were reunited with his uncle."

Wizard Arkwright, along with his uncle, a wizard known now only as the Arkower, had been the cause of all of the Castle's troubles. The Arkower and his rival, Wizard Bratsch, had started the war and created the plague that killed most of the griffin riders and almost all their griffins. The Arkower and Arkwright had broken the Eye of the Castle in two and sent half of it to Sleyne with Arkwright, out of sheer spite, because if they couldn't control the Castle, they didn't want anyone else to have it.

The Arkower had remained behind, still trying to gather his own army of griffins, though the griffins would have nothing to do with him. And Arkwright had done his best to erase the history of the Castle and keep others from finding out its secret, until Celie and her family had exposed his past and locked him away in the dungeons, which, until then, had been used as a cheese cellar.

"And now he's loose," Bran said grimly. "I've already sent a dove to the College of Wizardry to let them know he's escaped. The team of wizards they dispatched to transport him to Sleyne City should have been here days ago anyway!" He gave his poor hat another twist. "What next?"

"You're asking *us*?" King Glower said, goggling at his oldest child. "*You're* the Royal Wizard!"

"Where would he go?" Pogue asked before a family argument could break out. "Does he have a home? Where was he before he came here to cause trouble?"

"He's an itinerant wizard," Bran said.

"What does that mean?" Celie asked. She repeated the word "itinerant" to herself softly, sounding it out.

"It means he travels around, helping where he's needed," Bran explained. "He never was stationed in one particular place or had a position at any court."

"*Helping*," Rolf sneered.

"He was highly respected by the Wizards' Council," Bran said. He shrugged. "Because of the way he came and went, how were they to know he was several hundred years old and—"

"Evil?" Rolf supplied.

"Yes, evil," King Glower said. "Too evil to be caught. Where would he go? Not to Sleyne City and the College. He must have a home somewhere."

"Is it being in my Grath?" Lulath asked.

"Why would you think that?" Bran frowned in thought. "He's never mentioned Grath when I've spoken with him."

"Is this because of that village?" Celie asked, feeling a little surge of excitement. She'd been slumped against Rufus, feeling utterly dejected about the prospect of ever finding Arkwright, but now she straightened. "Do you think they'd hide him?"

"If they are being the people of which we are thinking they are being, I am thinking it might be yes," Lulath said, nodding eagerly.

"Someone help me understand what they're talking about," King Glower said, looking at Lilah and then Bran in appeal.

"Is that the village you were telling me about?" Bran's frown deepened. "We've no real proof, though."

"Children, please," King Glower said, looking pained. "What village?"

"Oh, our Celie, you are speaking this better than I," Lulath said, gesturing for her to proceed.

"Well," Celie said, trying not to look too pleased at being asked, "there's a village in Grath, on the sea, where they speak a very strange language. There is no other language like it in our world." She raised her eyebrows to see if her parents were following, and her father nodded. "They keep to themselves. No one ever leaves, and they don't like visitors, either. People have tried to learn the language, to trade with them, and they refuse. They have their own leaders, and they don't even pay taxes!"

"How is that possible?" Rolf looked outraged. "It's just one village! Can't your father do something, Lulath?"

"They are having this parchment from my many greats of a grandfather," Lulath said with a shrug. "On it is being agreed that they are being left of themselves, and they are not leaving their village or doing the attacking of others."

"No offense," Rolf said, "but I think that's a terrible idea! There's a village that is basically its own kingdom, just sitting in Grath?" He shook his head.

"We have *two* such villages in Sleyne," King Glower told him, the corners of his eyes crinkling in amusement. "One is a large farm for women who have taken holy orders and want to live in silence. The other is little more than a shrine, a well, and a single farmhouse, which is occupied by the last descendants of an ancient nation that existed before Sleyne. They just want to farm turnips and keep the shrine painted. Oh, and call themselves the Ailerites in honor of King Ailor the Last. I have no objection to that."

"What?" Rolf stared at their father. "But . . . that seems so . . . irresponsible."

"Why?" Bran smiled faintly. "Are you afraid a bunch of holy women are going to attack us and take the throne? For pity's sake, Rolf, they don't even wear shoes in the winter!"

"Why don't we give them some shoes?" Lilah said. "I think that's very bad of us!"

"They don't *want* shoes," King Glower said patiently. "They don't want anything but to be left alone." He shook his head. "Now, Celie, explain what this independent village has to do with Arkwright . . . ?"

"While we were in Hatheland," Celie continued, "Lulath became certain that the language we heard the wizards speaking is the one they speak in that village."

"I am traveling there at once ago," Lulath said. "I am wanting to learn of them, but they are telling me no, I must go back, making show with the hands, because they are not speaking my Grathian. But of among each other, I am hearing a speaking that is not dislike the one we heard of Wizard the Arkower and the Ethan."

Ethan was a young man from Hatheland who had begged permission to come with them to Sleyne. He now worked in the griffin stables, grooming and caring for the griffins as he'd been trained to do in his homeland, though he'd tried and failed several times to bond with a baby griffin.

"So, if Lulath is right," Celie finished, "that means that the people of that village are the griffin riders who survived. The griffins chased the unicorns to the sea, the riders followed them, the unicorns got on a ship, the griffins died, and the people who were left shut themselves off from the world."

"That is so odd that it must be true," King Glower said after a moment's deliberation. "And it's our best chance for finding out anything about Arkwright. He has to have been with them at some point. Even if he isn't there now, they might know where he would go to hide."

"Brilliant," Lilah said, clapping her hands. She turned to Celie with shining eyes. "You see? Now we *have* to go to Grath!"

"What joy is bringing me!" Lulath exclaimed, beaming at Lilah. "You must be coming to my Grath for the meeting of that family of mine, my only Lilah!" He reached out his long arms from his seat on the floor, and embraced Lilah around the knees, crushing her elaborate skirts.

"Yes," Lilah said, not seeming to notice the wrinkling of her gown. "Finally!" She ran her fingers through Lulath's gleaming hair, which was only a shade less gold than Juliet's fur.

"Oh, dear," Queen Celina murmured. "I thought the escaped wizard was complication enough."

"I'll be in the library," Pogue said, and left in disgust.

"Wait," King Glower said. "Now someone has to explain *this* to me. Immediately." He pointed to Lulath and Lilah and looked to his wife for help this time.

But it was Lulath who explained. He leaped to his feet, nearly knocking Lilah down in the process. Before she could stumble, he caught her up in his arms and held her high.

"Oh, My Our Majesty King Glower!" Lulath did a little spin while Lilah shrieked with laughter, her face bright red. "I am wanting, so very, to be having this our Lilah for my bride!"

"That's what I thought was happening," King Glower said, putting one hand to his forehead.

"May I? May it be so?" Lulath lowered Lilah tenderly to the floor, his eyes on her. She gave a little sigh and leaned against his chest.

King Glower waved one hand. "I'm fairly certain that nothing I can say will put a stop to this now," he said.

"Oh, Father!" Lilah said in horror. "You wouldn't say no!"

"Of course not, my dear," King Glower hurried to reassure her. "I was only joking. Let me assure you both that nothing would make me happier."

Juliet and Lorcan began rubbing their heads together, cooing, while Celie just stood and stared. Rufus butted her, and she put a hand on Bran's arm to steady herself.

"I don't want to leave the Castle," she told him.

"I don't think we're going to have a choice," Bran said, blinking rapidly at Lilah and Lulath, who still had their arms around each other.

"Ew," Rolf announced.

Chapter
3

⟨ornament⟩

Hiding was childish, but Celie didn't care. She wasn't about to sit in the throne room for one more day and watch Lilah and Lulath mooning over each other while her father sent off messages to Lulath's family and everyone buzzed about the pending betrothal.

"'Betrothal' is a stupid word," Celie said, and Rufus squawked in reply.

They were in the farthest reaches of the Castle, in what had been the old nursery. Celie figured that if someone did find her there, she could always claim that she had come to look for some old baby blankets for the griffins. Autumn was coming, and Rufus had a tendency to chew on her blankets at night.

"Betrothal," Celie said again, kicking at a trunk of old toys.

It wasn't that she didn't want Lulath and Lilah to get married. She loved Lilah, and she really liked Lulath. No, after all they'd been through together, she loved him, too. He was like a brother to her now—how could he not be?

But if they got married, Lilah would go live in Grath. The king and queen had already begun talking about who would go to Grath to announce the betrothal and for how many months.

Not days, not weeks, but months. And Celie was included in the party.

The wedding would take place in Sleyne, but royal weddings took time. There was a great deal of preparation to be made, and Lulath's family had to meet Lilah—and Queen Celina and even Rolf and Celie, apparently—and they had to decide terms of the marriage: how much land in Sleyne they would inherit, how much in Grath. Would Lulath be in line for the throne of Sleyne, or would Lilah give up her title, in favor of possibly being queen of Grath? This last item meant that a handful of people had to die, though, because Lulath was the third son, and fifth child, and it seemed that his older brothers and sisters all had children as well. But it had to be put in writing anyway, and approved by both families.

Lilah was getting her wish for a new wardrobe, both here in the Castle and in Grath. It seemed that, according to Lilah, she and Celie would need gowns suitable for traveling to Grath, then other gowns for their stay in Grath, and any other fashionable gowns, shoes, fans, or gloves they saw between the Castle and Lulath's home as well. Lilah was insistent that they could not look poor or outmoded in front of Lulath's family. And the seamstresses needed to start right away, because Lilah and Celie were leaving Castle Glower as soon as their gowns could be made.

Celie had been hoping that the Castle would object somehow, but it showed no signs of caring. She knew that she couldn't hide forever . . . well, she could probably hide in the Castle for at least a month . . . but she'd need food, water, and a reasonable excuse, so she knew she couldn't be gone long.

She could, however, hide for the afternoon, and avoid being measured for her gowns and hearing Lilah squeal over fabrics. Just for one afternoon.

Everyone was acting ridiculous, and now no one seemed to care that Arkwright was missing. Bran had sent out more doves, and he was planning to leave on his own in the next few days, to travel ahead of them to the College of Wizardry and then on to Grath. Members of the Council, backed by Castle guards, had been sent to the villages and cities of Sleyne to hunt for the escaped wizard as well.

Celie thought that leaving the Castle wouldn't be so bad if she were doing something important, like finding Arkwright. She'd offered to go, too, had proposed that she and Rolf and Pogue take a dozen guards and ride for Sleyne City, and her father had said no without even considering it. But traveling in state so that she could stand behind her sister while Lilah got married sounded too horrible for words.

"Beeee-troth-aaaal," Celie said again.

She idly flipped open the trunk that held some of their old toys. There was a leather ball that had belonged to Rolf lying on top, and Rufus immediately tried to grab it. He couldn't get his beak open far enough to bite it, though, so Celie took it out of the chest and started to throw it for him. Rufus went through a ball a week, since after fetching the ball for a few days he would try to tear it apart like a juicy ham. Celie bent down to see if there were any more balls in the chest, but only found a set of blocks and some puzzles. The chest was barely half-full: the queen had donated many of their old toys to families in the village, and Lilah still had her dolls, looking like new, lined up on a shelf in her room.

Celie's favorite childhood toy, a stuffed lion named Rufus, held pride of place in the middle of her bed. She used to feel self-conscious about keeping Rufus, but a year ago her old toy had become part of the spell that brought Lord Griffin briefly to Sleyne, where he attacked the murderous Prince Khelsh and saved Celie's life. Months later, Celie had named her real live griffin after the toy, then found the toy Rufus again in Hatheland, being kept in a run-down stable by Lord Griffin. The poor, grayish toy lion had been washed and mended and was viewed almost with reverence by the housekeeping staff. Consequently, Celie was no longer embarrassed when people saw him in her room.

"No more balls," she told Rufus the griffin, closing the lid of the trunk. She threw the one they'd found for him a few more times. "What's in here?"

She tried to keep her mind off the betrothal and subsequent departure from the Castle by looking through more trunks. She found some old clothes, quite a few early reading primers and scribbled-in schoolbooks with broken spines, and finally some blankets. She took out a few that were in fairly good shape, wondering why her mother would keep such things. She supposed they reminded Queen Celina of her children as babies, but some of them were little more than rags, and Celie couldn't see the point.

She tucked the blankets under one arm and closed the lid of the chest. Rufus had gotten the ball stuck in the corner of the room, behind the leg of a table, and she went over to help him, her gaze on the tapestry on the wall behind the table.

Celie considered herself an expert on the Castle's tapestries, now that they'd been to the Glorious Arkower and Hatheland, and realized that some of the tapestries had been made by one people, and some by another. Arkish tapestries were more stylized and the people looked very stiff, while the Hathelocke tapestries were very elaborate, with lots of curling vines and flowers. This was a Hathe-locke tapestry. It had griffins on it, as they all did, and she idly kicked Rufus's ball free as she felt the fine stitches of the tapestry. It was in very good repair, though dusty, and she decided to ask about moving it to her bedchamber. It wasn't doing any good here.

She couldn't remember seeing this one before, which was strange, since she'd spent the first years of her life in this very room. She decided that it must have been in Hatheland and just arrived with the rest of the Castle. There were a lot of new furnishings and even dishes and linens, now that the Castle was whole. Of course, none of them were actually *new*; they were the Castle's original goods, and most of them were old and battered.

Celie looked to the top of the tapestry to see how it was attached, wondering how much work it would be to take it down, air it, and rehang it. It had curtain rings at the top, she saw, and was hung on a rod. That was also strange. She pulled it sideways to see if it really moved like a curtain and found a door behind it. She was sure there hadn't been a door there when she was little. In fact, she was sure this wall had been home to a series of pictures of horses and dogs and deer, painted by one of their mother's cousins.

Celie had been trying to correct her atlas of the Castle since they'd returned from the Glorious Arkower, but the Castle was now more than twice as big as it had been, and she still wasn't done. And now here was yet another room she didn't know about! Setting down the blankets on the table nearby, Celie didn't hesitate to open the door.

To her disappointment, it was only more storage. Large bundles and crates, marked in a foreign language that was probably Hathelocke, though possibly Arkish—she would have to find out if Ethan could read it. She took a few steps into the room and peered around, to make sure she hadn't missed anything, but there weren't even any windows, and no other door. She turned to walk out and screamed.

Looming in the corner by the door was a griffin standing on its hind legs and wearing a crown!

Rufus came, screeching, to her rescue, but by the time he'd taken position in front of Celie she had already realized that the griffin was carved out of wood. It appeared to be a strange and slightly terrifying statue of rich dark wood, with touches of gilt lining the crown, eyes, and feathers. Rufus hissed at it, but Celie found that she liked it, once her heart slowed down.

"Maybe I'll put that in my room, too," she told him. "Or the throne room, if everyone starts being nice to me."

Rufus just hissed again.

Chapter
4

ᴦ⁓⁓ᴧ

Good heavens, Celie, do you know what this is?" Bran put both hands to his head, dislodging his round wizard's hat and scrubbing at his hair.

"A statue?" Celie asked uncertainly.

"Close. It's actually a figurehead," Bran said. "For a ship. A large one, judging by the size."

"A ship? A figurehead?" Celie gaped. She had not been expecting that.

"The Builder's ship," Ethan said in reverent tones. He'd been invited to come and see the goods in the storage room Celie had discovered, and translate any of the writings that he could. "I thought it was just a myth."

"Apparently not," Bran said. He ran his hands along the back of the griffin.

Celie moved around, raising the lamp she held higher, and saw what Bran had seen. The back of what she'd thought was a statue was a long, squared-off beam. There were marks where it had once been fastened to the prow of a ship, the wood scarred from being pried loose. The carved griffin's back arched, and his wings flared. Celie could imagine him poised on the front of a ship with golden sails.

"Tell us the myth," Celie said to Ethan. "Please," she added.

She had a hard time talking to Ethan. He had helped them escape from Hatheland, and from his onetime master, the Wizard Arkower, as well. Then Ethan had gathered up the eggs that were now nestled in the Castle's hatching towers, and hidden them from the Arkower until Celie and her friends could rescue them.

But Ethan had been a servant of the Arkower since he was younger than Celie, and he'd tried and failed three times to bond with a newborn griffin. The baby griffins, unwilling to eat from Ethan's hand and with no parents to care for them, had died. It made Celie uncomfortable to think about the griffins that had died, and how Ethan kept trying to bond with one, even when he knew that failure would mean their death.

"It's not a really exciting myth," Ethan said apologetically. "More like just another chapter in the life of the Builder. He built a ship on the shores of the lake, and when it was ready, he sailed it from the lake to the sea, and then on to exotic lands. He brought back two of his wives from that journey . . . I suppose you saw their likenesses in the tomb?" He looked at Celie, and she nodded.

Celie had been to the Tomb of the Builder, the first king of the Castle, in the Glorious Arkower. Celie and her companions had gone first out of curiosity, then to hide from the battling wizards, Arkower and Bratsch, and later to retrieve the griffin eggs that Ethan had hidden. Bran and her parents had been with her that last time and had seen the Tomb of the Builder with their own eyes.

The tomb was filled with treasure: weapons, jewels, rich clothing, and even food. It also contained statues in the likenesses of the Builder's five wives and two dozen children. The only actual bodies in the tomb belonged to the Builder and his griffin, who lay side by side at the far end of the long chamber.

"Well, anyway," Ethan said. "Two of his wives were from far-off lands, supposedly brought back on this ship. And then the ship was either sunk in a storm or just got old and was no longer fit to sail, depending on who tells the story." He shrugged.

"How do you sail a ship from a lake to the sea?" Celie frowned.

She had sailed on the now-poisoned lake and knew that it was very far from the ocean. They'd never even seen the ocean in that world, since it was several days' travel away.

"There used to be a wide river running from the lake to the ocean," Ethan said. "But there was an earthquake and a landslide or something that filled in part of it a few hundred years ago."

"It was probably the Arkower," Celie said darkly.

"No, it really was an earthquake," Ethan said. "It was before the Castle left, though apparently it did make the lake much easier for Arkwright to poison."

"Ugh," Celie said.

"What happened to the river hardly matters now," Bran said. "What does matter is that this is a magnificent piece, and we need to bring it to the throne room to show Father." He ran his hands over the griffin's wings. "Magnificent," he murmured.

"There appears to be more of the ship stored here," Ethan said. "This crate is marked as belonging to the captain's quarters. And that one says 'sails' on it."

"Even better," Bran said.

"I'll go get some men to help us move this," Ethan offered.

"Excellent. Thank you," Bran said.

After Ethan had left, Celie set her lamp down and paced around the crates, studying them. If they were all parts of the ship, then there was a great deal here. How large a ship had it been? Did it look like the ships Celie had seen pictures of?

"I've never been to the sea," she said, half to herself.

"You'll be in Grath in less than two months," Bran said. He grunted a little, trying to shift the figurehead himself. "The palace is right on the shore."

"Ugh," Celie said again.

Bran stopped admiring the wooden griffin and turned to her in surprise. "Don't you want to go to Grath?"

"Not particularly," she said, not caring that she sounded like she was pouting. "Not that anyone cares how I feel about it."

"But they . . . why should . . ." Bran appeared to be at a loss. Celie supposed that this sort of thing wasn't covered in classes at the College of Wizardry. "Lulath and Lilah are in love," he finally said, rather severely. "Aren't you happy for them? I thought you liked Lulath—who could possibly *not* like Lulath?"

"I adore Lulath," Celie said. "As you said, how could I not? Lulath is funny and kind and everything is exciting to him, which makes *him* exciting to be around. I'm very happy that he and Lilah are going to get married." But she didn't sound like she was. She heard it, and Bran did, too.

"Why don't you want Lilah to get married?" Bran gazed at her. "You're not jealous, are you?" His gaze sharpened. "How *much* do you adore Lulath?"

"What? No!" Celie glared at him. "And also: ew. I adore Lulath *like a brother*."

"Then why don't you want to go to Grath?" Bran asked. "I can't wait, personally, because I want to see how many cats, dogs, parrots, pygmy deer, and fancy rats his family can fit into one palace." He chuckled.

Lulath, with his four dogs and one griffin, was by no means the odd man out in his family. He had regaled them with stories about all his family's pets over the last year, including sharing the family secret that one of his sisters preferred cats to dogs. This appeared to be the greatest scandal that had happened in the Grathian royal family in many generations. Grath did sound like a happy and interesting place to visit.

To *visit.*

"I want to go to Grath . . . someday," Celie said slowly. "And I know that Lilah wants to go, too. I guess I didn't realize that she wanted to go so badly, because of Lulath . . ." She took a deep breath, and felt tears pricking her eyes. "And I didn't think she'd want to stay!"

"Stay?" Bran looked astonished. "You don't think she wants to stay there forever, do you? Does Father know? That's certainly going to make the marriage contracts more complicated! When did she tell you this?"

"Wait . . . what?"

"In here," Ethan said, and led a troop of manservants into the room.

"Celie, we need to talk," Bran said. Then he turned to the men. "Sorry to be a bother, but we really do need these crates carried down to the . . . well, not the throne room," he said.

"The Heart of the Castle," Celie put in. "What we used to call the holiday feasting hall."

They had started using it last spring to collect all the stories, tapestries, and maps they could find that related to griffins, before they learned that it had been the original throne room. Celie's father preferred the newer throne room, but the Heart had become a sort of all-purpose room for the royal family.

"Yes, that's an excellent idea," Bran said. "But this large fellow needs to be very carefully taken to the throne room." He rubbed his hand fondly over the griffin's beak. "My father will want to see it right away."

As the men got busy with the crates, Celie slipped out. She was sure that Bran wouldn't even notice. She was sure, too, that although she would get the credit for discovering the figurehead, it wouldn't matter. Her father and Bran would do what they wanted with it, without asking her. They always did. And they would just apologize later if they found out she was upset.

Assuming they took the time to even find out how she felt.

Chapter
5

⟨≈⟩

It was exactly as Celie predicted.

Her parents complimented her on her cleverness at finding the hidden storeroom, and then everyone began discussing what to do next, without bothering to see if Celie had any ideas. Pogue and Ethan were tasked with unpacking the crates and seeing what was inside. Bran was to arrange the figurehead in the corner of the throne room, and use magic to make sure that it wouldn't accidentally fall over. It was not as sturdy on its base as it had appeared when propped in the corner of the storeroom, and the king didn't want it to topple forward and hurt someone, or be damaged.

"Just make sure you don't stick it to the wall permanently," the king said, a smile stretching across his face. He looked over at Lilah and Lulath, who were holding hands. They were always holding hands now. "I believe that it might make a very fine wedding gift . . . provided we can reattach it to a ship."

"Oh, Father!" Lilah dropped Lulath's hand and ran to hug King Glower. "A ship? For us?"

"Now what fineness is this?" Lulath also embraced the king. "What magnificence! A gift of a king for sureness!"

The court erupted into chatter and even some cheers. The Glower family all rushed to congratulate Lilah and Lulath on their good fortune in getting a ship as a gift. All of them, except Celie.

"Breathe, Celie, breathe," someone whispered in her ear.

She felt a warm, calloused hand take hold of one of her clenched fists and gently unbend her fingers. She managed to unclench her other fist and put her hand on Rufus's back to steady herself.

"It's not fair, Pogue," she whispered.

"I know," he whispered back.

"I found the figurehead, and the crates, and now my father is just giving them away without asking," she said.

"I know."

"And they're going to go away to Grath and never come back!" To her embarrassment, tears burst from her eyes as she said it.

"Oh, oh, no, they're not," Pogue said gently. "They'll come back."

"They will?" Celie looked up at him in surprise.

33

"No one's even bothered to tell you, have they?" Pogue said, still talking in a near whisper. "They'll go to Grath once a year for a state visit. And sail in their ship around the bay while they're there, I suppose."

He sounded faintly bitter, and Celie remembered that, until about six months ago, Pogue had been flirting outrageously with Lilah at every opportunity—something that Lilah had definitely enjoyed. And now that Pogue had been knighted and was Bran's assistant, rather than his father's apprentice at their blacksmith shop in the village, he had probably hoped to be taken more seriously by Lilah. But instead she'd turned her affections to Lulath.

Celie realized that Pogue was still holding her hand, and gave his hand a comforting squeeze.

"They'll live here?" She felt more tears prickle her eyes, but this time, tears of relief.

"I can't believe no one's told you," Pogue muttered. "Of course they will! Lilah is third in line to the throne, behind Rolf and then you, you knew that, right?"

Celie nodded. Rolf was the heir to the throne of Sleyne, and had briefly been crowned King Glower the Eightieth last year, when Prince Khelsh of Vhervhine had tried to take over the Castle. After they'd gotten rid of Khelsh, Celie's father had written an exact list of succession, putting Celie next after Rolf, and Lilah after Celie. Bran, as a wizard, was not allowed to inherit a throne, so Celie supposed that one of their cousins on their father's side would be after Lilah, if it came to that. Of course, after Rolf married and had children, the succession would change to include them.

"Lilah's third in line for the throne of Sleyne, but Lulath is *twelfth* in line for the throne of Grath," Pogue went on. "Plus: two of his older brothers' wives are expecting babies. That means that Lilah outranks him. It's more important for them to be part of the court here than there."

"Oh," Celie said, feeling warmth spread through her body. "Oh. They're coming back."

"I can't believe no one told you," Pogue said again.

"Well, I may have been hiding," Celie admitted.

Pogue laughed out loud.

The family heard, and Lilah turned around.

"What's so funny?" She was radiant with happiness, but then she saw Celie and her face clouded. "Where on earth have you been? You've missed two fittings for your new gowns!"

Half the court turned to look at Celie.

"If I'd been at the fittings, I wouldn't have found the figurehead for *your ship*," Celie retorted.

"Celie!" Queen Celina chided her. "Manners!"

Celie opened her mouth, realized that she was still very close to crying, and closed it again. She couldn't even summon an apology for Lilah: and why did she need to apologize? Lilah had just scolded her in front of the entire court for missing a stupid gown fitting, and no one had even bothered to thank her for the generous gift of the figurehead for what would be her very own ship!

Pogue let go of her hand, but only so he could put it on her shoulder. "Your Majesty," he said politely to Queen Celina. "I think this has been a very . . . exciting . . . few days for everyone. Perhaps you and your daughters should have some private time to talk?"

"Pogue Parry, are you trying to tell my mother what to do?" Lilah demanded, but Queen Celina shushed her, looking thoughtful.

"What a fine idea, Sir Pogue," the queen said. "It's nearly dinner, but I haven't even had lunch yet. Celie, why don't you and Lilah come to my solar and we'll have something to eat and we can rest and talk?"

"Lulath, why don't you come with us?" Lilah said, smiling up at him.

But Lulath, despite all his exuberance and extravagant clothes, was no fool. "Now, my Lilah, I am thinking that this is being the time to talk to your mother and your Celie with only the three of you." He smiled. "And I am thinking this is the time to be seeing what other joys of shipbuilding our Celie is finding!"

He put both arms around Celie and gave her a rib-cracking hug. Celie's resolution not to cry completely crumbled, and she bawled all over Lulath's silk-covered shoulder.

Chapter
6

⟨≈⟩

Celie did her best to explain that she loved Lulath, and was happy for him and for Lilah, but she couldn't stop crying.

"We just got back to the Castle," she sobbed, while a wide-eyed maid set tea and scones on the table in the queen's solar, a beautiful room with wide windows that overlooked the gardens. "I don't want to leave again! What if something bad happens? And you know that we'll never find Arkwright—with all the things for the wedding, how can we even pretend we're trying to find him?"

She didn't mention that she had wanted to keep the figurehead to herself. She knew that it was a selfish wish, but sometimes she just wanted to have something for herself. A secret. A gift from the Castle. Rufus had been a gift from the Castle, one that was just for her, but Bran had known about him only an hour after Rufus had hatched, and Pogue had found out a few weeks later. Now there were dozens of griffins at court, and most people couldn't even tell them apart.

"So you're *not* happy for me?" Now Lilah looked like she might cry. "I don't understand, Celie. Why are you doing this?"

"Lilah," the queen said patiently. "Calm yourself. I know exactly what Celie is saying." Queen Celina put a hand on Celie's arm and one on Lilah's. "Not everyone loves excitement and change as much as you do, Lilah. Not everyone is bored by life in the Castle."

"I'm not bored," Lilah protested, then stopped short. "Well, all right, I am. But it wasn't boring to go Hatheland, and I didn't exactly love that little adventure!"

"Exactly," their mother said. "In the past year you've thought that Daddy, Bran, and I were dead, thought that awful Khelsh had killed the Castle, found out that griffins are real, and traveled to another world. That's a lot to take in, especially for someone as young as Celie."

Celie, whose tears had been drying as she heard her mother's words, scowled. She thought her mother understood, but no, she just thought Celie was being childish.

There was a faint scratching sound coming from the wooden paneling, and Celie looked around, momentarily distracted. Her mother saw her looking, and shrugged.

"I thought there'd be fewer mice, with so many griffins in residence," the queen said. "Nothing to worry about, though."

"I suppose you think I need a nap," Celie grumbled.

Queen Celina sighed. "No, that's not what I meant at all. I think we all need a rest. We all need some boring time. But it's just not going to happen."

Now Lilah's tears started in earnest. "I knew it! You think I'm too young to be married! You're going to make me wait until I'm old and gray and Lulath doesn't love me anymore!"

"Oh, for heaven's sake!" The queen threw up her hands. "I don't think either of you is listening to me! I'm just trying to explain why all our emotions are very close to the surface. Even mine, and your father's! A lot is going on, and we haven't had a great deal of time to cope, and we're all reacting in different ways. Celie is hiding from her fittings; you, Lilah, are being very dramatic; and your father wants to build a ship despite knowing nothing about ships or the ocean!"

Celie looked curiously at her mother. "How about you? How are you . . . coping?" It had just occurred to her that she hadn't seen much of her mother lately, and she wondered where the queen had been and what she'd been doing.

"I've been studying our griffin friends," the queen said lightly. She smiled over at Lady Griffin, Rufus's mother, who was lying near one of the tall windows, soaking the sun into her golden hide.

"She's so beautiful." Lilah sighed. "I'm sure that Juliet will look just like her when she's grown. I wonder if they're related."

"It's very likely," the queen agreed.

Celie thought that her mother looked relieved to have had the attention diverted from her to the griffin. She wondered if that was *all* her mother was doing. Queen Celina was the daughter of the old Royal Wizard, and she had enough talent to have been accepted by the College of Wizardry but had decided not to go. Lately their mother had shown herself to be increasingly aware of the magic around them, and seemed to spend most of her time in the oldest parts of the Castle library, or alone in her solar.

The queen caught Celie studying her and smiled again, disarmingly. "Are you feeling better now, Celie darling?"

"I suppose," Celie said. It did feel good to cry for a bit. But it didn't really change the fact that the ship was still going to be built in Grath, the figurehead taken away from her, and she was going to be wearing a lot of uncomfortable new clothes very soon.

"Well, *I'm* not feeling any better," Lilah declared.

Celie and Queen Celina both turned to her. She'd been cooing happily at Juliet and Lady Griffin, her tears dried on an elegantly embroidered handkerchief. But now she did look unhappy.

"What's the matter?" the queen asked.

"I thought Celie would want to be with me on this new adventure," Lilah said.

"Getting married?" the queen said, puzzled, before Celie had a chance to say the same thing. "I would imagine that you'd want Lulath with you on this particular *adventure*, not Celie. And Lulath is with you body and soul." The queen smiled.

"I mean the ship," Lilah said, waving a hand in front of her face to toss aside the queen's rather lighthearted remark. "It's really the ship that's gotten to you, Celie, isn't it?"

Celie nodded.

"I've talked about this with Celie several times since we returned from Hatheland," Lilah declared. "And I thought Celie would support me, help me win over Father and Lulath's family. That's why I was really upset when Celie started . . . crying . . . over that chunk of wood."

"It's not just a chunk of wood," Celie protested. "It's a *piece* of the *Castle*."

"It's a piece of the Castle that could help us find the unicorns," Lilah retorted. "Unless you don't want to help me look for them anymore?"

"I do," Celie said slowly. "I just . . . didn't think that we would go right away. I didn't think that we'd be going as part of you getting married and maybe living in Grath . . . I didn't think that . . . I don't know, I just don't . . ."

"Yes, Lilah, I'm with Celie," the queen said, frowning. "You want to do what now?"

41

"Find the unicorns," Lilah said. It was the only thing she cared as much about as her engagement, and Celie did feel a little bad about not being as enthusiastic. "We know that there must be unicorns, because the stories all end with them being chased off by the griffins. And the stories about the griffins are true; therefore, the unicorns are real. And we can assume that they really have been exiled to Larien. I want to find them!"

"But we can hardly bring them back," Celie argued. "Since there *are* griffins here again, and they ate the unicorns last time. If you bring unicorns back here, the griffins will just attack them!"

"Yes, Lilah, what is your intention? I'm not really sure adding more animals to our growing menagerie is a good idea. I'm half-afraid one of Lulath's dogs is going to disappear some night," Queen Celina said, shaking her head.

"We've been training the griffins very carefully," Lilah said. "You've seen Lorcan and Juliet playing with the girls! They get along just fine now!"

Celie wondered when Lilah had started calling Lulath's dogs "the girls." Perhaps if Celie had paid attention to such things, Lilah and Lulath's engagement would not have come as quite so much of a shock.

"And besides," Lilah continued, "I hadn't actually thought about bringing one of them back. I just want to make sure they're all right." But she wore a sly expression.

"Delilah," their mother said in a warning voice, clearly also seeing that look.

"All right, I want one," she admitted. "*One*. Lulath has *four* dogs, and is talking about getting another, and he has a griffin, too! Why can't I have a griffin and a unicorn?"

"Because one would eat the other?" Celie suggested.

"Because this isn't a competition," the queen responded almost at the same time. "You shouldn't feel the need to compete with your husband in the matter of pets, or anything else!"

"Oh, really? And who always has to beat Daddy at the midsummer games every year?" Lilah demanded.

"That's all in good fun," the queen protested. "And no one is in danger of being eaten!" The queen shook her head. "I can't believe you were thinking of doing something like that . . . when were you going to tell us?"

"I was going to have Celie help me win you over," Lilah said, giving Celie a reproachful look. "She told me she wanted to go, too, and I knew you'd let her do anything she wanted. She always gets what she wants," Lilah grumbled.

"What?" Celie stared at her sister in astonishment. "Me? I'm not the one who's getting married far too young, and being given a ship that someone else discovered the materials for!"

"*Aha!*" Lilah shouted, pointing a manicured finger at Celie. "You're jealous! You're jealous because we're going to take a piece of your precious Castle without your permission!"

"Delilah, that was quite rude!" their mother said.

43

"It's not *my* Castle," Celie said, but couldn't muster much conviction.

That was almost exactly how she felt. She wasn't jealous of Lilah and Lulath getting a lot of attention: if anything, she was glad. She preferred to wander the halls of the Castle alone or with Rufus for company. But she was jealous of the fact that her discoveries were always taken away from her so quickly. The moment she found a new room, the rest of the Castle's residents would start filing through it to have a look. Even with Rufus, Bran had only helped her keep him a secret because the Castle actively tried to stop anyone else from seeing the griffin.

Lilah opened her mouth to say something, but closed it again when she saw the expression on Queen Celina's face. The queen didn't speak for a moment, either, but held up a hand to signal that she was thinking.

"Celie is right: this is all moving much too fast. And something else is troubling me. The last time Celie found something in the Castle, which the Castle seems to have put there specifically for her to find, it was Rufus. Perhaps your father should not have been so quick to promise the ship to you and Lulath," the queen said, tapping her lips.

"Mother!" Lilah actually put her hands in her hair, mussing the carefully arranged curls in distress. "You can't take back a gift! Not one that Father gave in public, and to a foreign prince! Wars have been fought over insults like this!"

44

"Please stop being so dramatic." Queen Celina sighed. "It does look bad to take back a gift, so we won't, though I doubt Lulath's father is going to declare war on us—at least not before the betrothal contract is even signed!

"But we do have to consider that, if this figurehead is part of the Castle, the Castle may have plans for it."

"Like going to find the unicorns it scared away," Lilah offered, innocently smoothing her hair.

"Or being used as a scratching post for baby griffins," her mother countered. "Either way, we are going to slow things down a bit. Celie, you will start coming to your fittings, because you do need new gowns." Her expression softened. "But it will be some time before you leave the Castle, and we will make sure that you are consulted on all matters concerning ships, journeys, and the Castle, all right?"

Celie nodded, not trusting her voice. She wanted to include news about Arkwright in that list, but didn't dare.

"As for you, miss," Queen Celina said sternly to Lilah. "You need to start acting like a young lady about to be married, and less like a spoiled girl who just wants presents."

"Mother, I—"

Bran threw open the door and leaned inside. "Is everyone in here all sorted out?" He rushed on without waiting to hear their answer. "Doesn't matter—there's an egg hatching, and if you want to watch, you'll follow me."

Chapter
7

⁓꣠⁓

This was the first egg to hatch in the Castle since griffins had returned to Sleyne. Celie and her companions had brought half a dozen eggs from Hatheland, along with the fully grown griffins, all of them mated pairs, but there were only four hatching towers. The eggs that Ethan had judged would hatch first had been put in the towers; the rest were in nests in one of the griffin stables. Most of the griffins had recognized their own eggs and were taking care of them, but two of the eggs were orphans, thanks to Wizard Arkwright's uncle, the Arkower. He had killed adult griffins and stolen their eggs as part of his plan to raise a griffin army.

The Arkower had also tried to bond with dozens of griffins, as had his followers, and all those newly hatched griffins had died. No one knew how baby griffins selected the person they bonded with, and they didn't have to bond with anyone at all, but there had been something lacking in the Arkower and his followers. Perhaps they were too greedy, too power-hungry, and the young griffins had sensed it and refused them. And because the Arkower had separated them from their parents, the little griffins had died of hunger, since they would only accept food from their parents or their bonded human.

That horrified everyone in the Castle who heard about it, so King Glower had made a declaration: All subjects might apply to bond with a griffin, with the understanding that if a griffin didn't bond with them, they were to abide by the beast's choice, and not try to steal an egg or a hatchling. At every hatching, the king would draw the names of a handful of candidates from a basket.

When Celie and her mother and sister arrived at the tower, they found that the selected persons included two Castle guards, a Councilor by the name of Lord Sefton, and Rolf. The four candidates were standing in a line under the watchful gaze of the egg's father, who was pacing between them and his offspring.

"How lucky for you, darling," the queen had said, kissing Rolf on the cheek. "I'm so glad that your name was called; I know how eager you are!"

Rolf scuffed his toe against the floor. "Well, technically it was Micah."

"Who's Micah?" The queen looked around, puzzled.

"From the village," Pogue said. He was helping Ethan arrange baskets of food along one side of the tower, under the approving gaze of the mother griffin. "The baker's son?"

"Oh, that darling boy with the dimples," Queen Celina said. "But then why didn't he come?"

"He came into the main hall, took one look at Lord Griffin, and turned green," Pogue told her. "He asked if they were all so scary."

"And I said, they're not scary, they're wonderful," Rolf said, taking up the story. "But just then Lord Griffin let out a screech, and Micah told me he'd changed his mind, and I could have his place." Rolf shrugged. "So here I am."

"We will keep young Micah's name in the basket," the king said. He was standing at the far side of the tower, watching the egg keenly. "He might change his mind again, once he gets used to them."

"I don't want anyone to think I scared him off, or pulled rank," Rolf said in a low voice.

"Seems fitting to me," one of the guards said. "Delighted as I am to have been chosen, I think the Crown Prince deserves first crack."

The others all nodded, and Rolf looked cheered.

"Speaking of cracks," Bran said.

They turned their attention to the egg, which was now rocking back and forth in its nest of moss and twigs. The griffin parents began to flap their wings and coo encouragement. Celie slid along the wall, staying clear of the wings and the rocking, and sat in the wide windowsill beside her father.

The agitated griffin parents-to-be screamed at any other griffins that attempted to enter the tower, so Celie sent Rufus to wait in the solar with his mother. At least, that's where Celie had told him to go, and she hoped that he'd understood. She peeked out the window, and though she saw a few other griffins sunning themselves on the roof of another tower, none of them was Rufus. Celie hoped he would stay out of trouble.

Of course, now that her mother had reminded her that Lulath's little dogs would make a tasty morsel for a griffin, she was more concerned about letting Rufus roam the Castle unsupervised. She turned to ask her father if he'd seen Lulath, and more importantly, Lulath's girls, but the prince himself entered the room.

"How the excitement stirs the air!" Lulath announced as he leaped into the room. He threw his arms around Lilah and lifted her off the ground. "Can you smell the happening?"

"Yes," Lilah squealed. "Please put me down!"

The griffin parents squalled, and Lilah and a temporarily subdued Lulath took their places against the wall. Celie tried to signal to Lulath to ask if his dogs were safely tucked away in his rooms—where they slept in a canopied bed on velvet cushions brought with him from Grath— but the egg was holding all the prince's attention.

Soon it held Celie's attention, too. Griffin hatchings were always dramatic. The eggs rocked harder and harder, sometimes standing on end. Rufus's egg had rocked, cracked all over, and then he'd stopped moving. When Celie had crept closer to make sure he was all right, the shell had exploded and the jagged pieces had almost struck her in the face.

"I am all in a mist, it is so the beautiful memory of my Lorcan when his egg was cracked," Lulath announced. Lorcan had leaped from his shell and made a beeline for Lulath. No amount of coaxing deterred him from the prince, though a young Arkish man had been offering him food and begging him to bond.

Celie found that she, too, was a bit teary-eyed. Looking across the room, she saw Lilah holding tight to one of Lulath's arms, and on his other side, her mother fondly patted his shoulder. Really, it would be fun to have him as a part of the family. As long as he and Lilah lived in the Castle, where they belonged.

"Here it comes," Ethan announced.

His eyes were fixed on the egg, and his expression was strained. Since he had tried several times without success to bond with a griffin in his homeland, which he still called the Glorious Arkower, having been taught to hate Hatheland and the Hathelockes all his life, Ethan insisted that he wasn't going to try to bond with another. He only wanted to help them all in their new home. He

50

was waiting now, ready to help whoever was lucky enough to be accepted by the baby griffin.

And he was right. The egg rocked twice more. The griffin parents' screaming changed to a low, throaty crooning, and the egg split down the middle. In the goopy wreckage of egg sat a large baby griffin, looking startled. It opened its mouth and let out a cry, and its parents rushed to reassure it.

"That is the ugliest thing I've ever seen," King Glower whispered to Celie. "Imagine it turning into one of those!" He pointed to the adult griffins.

Celie giggled. "Rufus looked like he was put together wrong. His wings and tail were too big for him," she whispered back.

"The paws on this one are enormous," her father said. "If it grows into those, it's going to be as big as the king!"

Celie watched for a moment as the parents cuddled their baby, rubbing their rounded eagle heads against the newborn's. Her father was right, though: this one was definitely bigger than the other three babies she'd seen, and its lion-like hind paws were simply enormous.

Its initial cries of distress quieted, but then it began the mewing sound that Celie knew meant hunger. She whispered to her father that it was time to feed the baby, and the king nodded at Ethan. Ethan handed a seed cake to each of the prospective griffin riders. They all stood around awkwardly, holding the cakes in limp hands. Then Rolf squatted down and held his out on a flat palm, the way you would offer a carrot to a horse. The other hopefuls followed suit, and the griffin parents drew back a little, nudging their baby toward the men.

The baby griffin turned away, crying. Celie saw the blood drain from Ethan's face. Ethan had stood by and watched as so many newly hatched griffins rejected riders, and then died, refusing to eat. Celie gripped her father's hand, squeezing as hard as she could and feeling a sharp stab of sympathy for Ethan. At least the parents would take over in a moment, and they would feed the baby. They wouldn't let it starve—it just wouldn't have a rider. And there was nothing wrong with that.

The hopeful riders crept closer, holding out the seed cakes. One of them was clucking his tongue, like he was calling a horse or a dog. Rolf whistled to get the little creature's attention, and it cocked its head, but backed up rather than take the offered cake. Its crying was growing in intensity, and the parents were stirring, also distressed.

Pogue squatted down and silently put some seed cakes near the parents, so that they could give them to the baby if they had to. As he straightened, he lost his balance a little and fell to one knee, muttering a curse. The baby griffin shrieked in surprise and spun around, falling on its beak.

"Sorry," Pogue said, pushing the seed cakes closer.

He straightened and backed away, but the baby griffin

scrabbled across the floor after him. It knocked the seed cake aside with one frantic claw, and kept on crying and crawling toward Pogue.

"Uh-oh," he said.

"Give it the cake," Lilah said, her brow creased with worry.

"I'm not supposed to," Pogue said, sounding almost as frantic as the griffin. At the sound of his voice, the baby griffin let out another cry, and began trying to reach Pogue with even greater determination.

"Friend Sir Pogue," Lulath said, flapping his hands to encourage Pogue. "The griffin is of the choosing, and the choosing is of you!"

"Give it the cake," Rolf said, his voice rough. He backed away from the griffin, then tossed his seed cake over the griffins. It struck Pogue in the chest, and Pogue caught it reflexively before it fell to the floor.

The newly hatched griffin was leaping around at Pogue's feet now, trying to snap the seed cake out of his hands. Every second leap it fell on its face or got a claw caught in one of its wings and toppled sideways, only to rise and try again. Pogue looked too stunned to help it.

"Give it the cake, lad," King Glower called out. "Quick, now!"

"It's not supposed to be me," Pogue protested.

"But it is you," Rolf said, and Celie could hear how much effort it was taking for him not to cry.

At last Pogue bent down and offered the cake to the baby griffin. With a cry of sheer delight it grabbed the cake and ate it in two bites, and then it began to rub itself against Pogue, cooing even as it searched his pockets for more food. The other hopeful riders, all looking just a bit disappointed, filed past and handed Pogue their cakes, which he fed to the griffin one after another.

The griffin parents crowded around Pogue, buffeting him with their wings and clicking their beaks in approval. Pogue crouched between them, looking stunned and feeding the hungry baby, which was trying to climb inside his tunic and eat at the same time. Pogue's face had gone from shocked to elated, and with his free hand, he shakily stroked the little griffin's head.

"A griffin," he said softly.

"A fine griffin," the king agreed.

"It's going to be *huge*," Bran said. "I think it's male."

Rolf plunged his hands in his pockets, nodded once, and then went out. Queen Celina made a little sympathetic noise and followed him. Pogue looked up, his expression clouding again.

"There was nothing you could have done," King Glower said, guessing what was troubling both Rolf and Pogue. "Rolf knows that."

"It's hard, I'm sure," Bran said. "But he'll be fine. And there are three other eggs I predict will hatch this week. Rolf will have his chance."

"But the lottery," Lilah said. "What if his name isn't drawn?"

"The lottery won't work," Bran said. "Clearly." He waved a hand at Pogue. "Pogue was the one this griffin wanted, and his name wasn't even in there, was it?"

"I put it in and took it back out," Pogue admitted. "I thought it seemed . . . greedy. I spend a lot of time at the Castle and with the griffins already."

"See?" Bran shook his head. "We're going to have to file anyone who might like a griffin through the room next time, have them all offer the hatchling a cake. They need more than four people to choose from. And those of us who don't want one or already have one should just stay away, so that there's less confusion."

"It sounds like chaos," King Glower said, looking unsure.

"But it will give the hatchlings the most options," Bran said.

Everyone turned and looked at Celie to see if she approved. She blinked, and then remembered that she'd had a griffin longer than anyone else, and as such was considered the expert.

"It makes sense," she said after a moment's hesitation.

"I'll announce the new rules tomorrow," King Glower said, as though Celie had been the deciding vote. Which, she realized, she had been. Her father turned back to Pogue and smiled. "What will you name him? I should also announce your good fortune."

"Bronze Arrow," Pogue said without hesitation. "Arrow for short."

"You're worse than Bran!" Celie blurted out, then put one hand over her mouth, embarrassed.

Bran, who had suggested names like Proudclaw and Goldenwings for Rufus, blushed.

"I think it's a fine name," King Glower said, giving Celie a faintly reproachful look.

Pogue hunched his shoulders. "It just suits him, all right?" he muttered.

"It does," Lilah agreed.

"It is being the finest of names!" Lulath cried.

"I'm really sorry," Celie said, contrite. "It's a lovely name." She supposed she couldn't make everyone name their griffins normal, sensible things like Rufus. And she had to admit that Lilah had done a very good job in naming Juliet.

"Oooh, it's another one," Ma'am Housekeeper said from the doorway. "Well, keep it out of my linens!" She sounded less than delighted to find another griffin in the Castle.

"Of course, Ma'am Housekeeper," the king said. "Has there been a problem with the griffins?"

"Them, or some very large rats, Your Majesty," she said bitterly. "I've come to speak to you about that, if you are done here. I've had outside of enough!"

Chapter
8

———❦———

Let's leave Sir Pogue and his new griffin to get to know each other," King Glower said. "Celie, would you mind coming along? To see if you think it's the griffins?"

Celie had been watching Pogue and the griffins and listening with half an ear to her father and the housekeeper. Now she gave them her full attention.

"Griffins chewing the linens?" she asked. Rufus was awful about chewing things he shouldn't, but—other than Celie's blankets—he was mostly interested in shoes, and Lorcan and Juliet showed the same tendencies.

"Not chewing," Ma'am Housekeeper said. "Stealing."

"What?" Celie followed her father and the housekeeper down the stairs from the hatching tower, face screwed up in confusion. "Stealing?"

"There's been food missing from the kitchens, Cook says," Ma'am Housekeeper told them. "And linens from the closets. A few other things, my girls say. Misplaced, moved, that sort of thing. They hear them scrabbling about, but can't seem to catch the beasts in the act."

Her tone was frosty. Ma'am Housekeeper was very strict. Even the most royal of guests soon learned to stay on her good side, and not make unreasonable demands of her staff or scuff the furniture. Ma'am Housekeeper kept a careful inventory of all the goods in the Castle, and knew precisely how many towels there were and whether they were in the laundry or neatly folded in a cupboard.

Cook was of a far more generous and easygoing nature, but she also kept her kitchens with precision. Food was given out gladly in the kitchens, but it never "went missing." This was serious indeed.

"What sort of food?" Celie asked.

The younger griffins favored fruit and seeds, while the older ones liked meat more. They also had certain preferences. Both Juliet and Lady Griffin enjoyed drinking milk, but none of the others would touch it. And Lorcan and Rufus had a fondness for sweets that led them to try to snatch cakes and sweetmeats out of the hands of people at dinner. It would help her figure out which griffin was guilty, if she knew what had been taken.

"A loaf of bread, a cheese, a bottle of wine, a basket of dates," the housekeeper recited. "And I'm missing half a dozen towels, and now two wool blankets and two sheets!"

58

Celie stopped walking. They were just at the bottom of the stairs, and headed toward the corridor that held the long row of closets where the linens were stored. But Celie didn't need to see them. She knew that it hadn't been a griffin.

"A loaf of bread . . . one loaf?" she asked.

The housekeeper nodded.

"And a bottle of wine?"

"And a wheel of cheese and a basket of dates."

"The basket, too?" Celie asked.

"The basket, too," Ma'am Housekeeper said darkly.

The king had also stopped, and when he looked at Celie, she could tell that her father had just had the same thought.

"Griffins didn't take the food," Celie said.

"I beg your pardon, Your Highness?"

"If griffins had taken the food, they would have taken all the bread they could snatch," Celie told her. "And they don't drink wine . . . besides which, they couldn't even carry the bottle!"

"Hmm," Ma'am Housekeeper said.

"Were the linens disturbed, as though an animal had grabbed them?" King Glower asked, arms folded over his chest and a thoughtful expression on his face.

"They were taken very carefully," the housekeeper admitted. "I doubt very much that a less careful person would have noticed they were gone. Certainly none of my girls noticed!" The look on her face made Celie very glad she wasn't one of the housekeeper's girls. "I was just checking the blankets, getting ready to change the bedding in the Councilors' bedchambers, when I found that some were missing!"

"If a griffin wanted to make a nest with the towels, it would have torn the closet apart," Celie said. "There would have been scratches from its talons on the doors of the cupboards, and it probably would have dropped some of the things on its way."

"You mean to say a person did this, and not one of those animals?" Ma'am Housekeeper looked appalled that a human would have tampered with her stores.

"It looks that way," the king said gravely. "But who?"

Celie knew. She could feel the answer vibrating the stones beneath her feet. The Castle seemed to pause, to wait and see if she would say it aloud.

"Arkwright," Celie said in a small voice.

"What's that, my dear?" King Glower had started down the corridor to take a closer look at the linen cupboards.

"Arkwright," Celie said, louder. "It was Arkwright."

"Oh, I hardly think . . . Bran is sure he's gone to Grath," King Glower said.

"How could he be sure?" Celie argued. "No one saw Arkwright leave! He could be right here in the Castle, hiding from us! He'd need food, and bedding, and now he's taken it."

"It's not possible," King Glower said, but he sounded like he was trying to convince himself, rather than arguing with Celie.

"That awful old wizard is loose in this Castle?" Ma'am Housekeeper was as close to rattled as Celie had ever seen her. "Living in the walls like a rat? We need to smoke him out!" She put one hand on a cupboard door and opened it, waving a hand at the shelves that were presumably lighter by two blankets and two sheets, though Celie could not tell.

When Celie was done studying the sheets and blankets that remained, she looked at the housekeeper, and saw that Ma'am Housekeeper was looking back at her, expectant.

So was King Glower.

"Me?" Celie squeaked. "You want *me* to find him?"

King Glower shook himself. "What? Of course not! That's a job for the Royal Wizard! I was just . . . thinking for a moment."

"We need to stop thinking and *do* something," Celie said. Her feet were tingling unbearably now. "We need to—"

The door to the cupboard next to them thumped, as though someone had rattled the latch. Celie stopped short and turned to look. The stones of the corridor heaved, making both Celie and her father take a few stumbling steps closer to that cupboard.

"What's happening?" Ma'am Housekeeper cried, clutching at the open door of the robbed cupboard to keep her balance.

"Something's amiss," King Glower said.

As if this were a signal, the door to the cupboard burst open, and a body fell out. Celie and Ma'am Housekeeper both screamed, and King Glower shouted out a curse that would have impressed the coachman.

It was a young woman, about four years older than Celie, wearing the gown and apron of one of the Castle staff. She was pale as chalk, and her dark braids were half-unraveled, her hair wrapping around her face and neck like waterweeds.

"It's Maisy," Ma'am Housekeeper said, when her scream had died away. She was clutching her chest, her face nearly as white as the maid's. "I sent her down to count the blankets this morning. I came myself because I thought she was shirking!"

"What's happened to her?" Celie said.

There was no sign of a wound.

King Glower knelt by the girl and gently straightened her crumpled form so that she was lying on her back. Celie braced herself to see a knife or an arrow . . . but there was nothing. She looked like she was asleep.

"Your Majesty? I heard screaming!" Lord Sefton, the Councilor who had just been trying to bond with the newly hatched Arrow, came running around the corner with his black robes held out of the way. At his heels came a pair of footmen, looking equally concerned.

"Get the Royal Wizard at once," Celie's father ordered. "He was in the western hatching tower!"

"You heard the king!" Lord Sefton said, delegating to one of the footmen. He hurried to kneel beside King Glower. "Please, allow me." He felt the girl's wrists and then her neck. "Her heart is beating, but only just," he whispered. "What happened to her?"

"She's alive?" Celie gasped.

"It would seem so," Lord Sefton said.

"Praise be!" Ma'am Housekeeper clapped her hands. "Do you think it was *him*?" She rolled her eyes meaning-fully.

"I can think of no one else it could be," King Glower said.

"Who?" Lord Sefton asked.

"Arkwright," Celie said.

"He's still here?" Lord Sefton's eyes bulged in horror.

"Summon the guards," King Glower said to the other footman. "They can start searching from here."

But Celie knew that Arkwright was long gone. The girl had been sent in the morning to check the blankets. He wouldn't be anywhere near this corridor now, and it was useless to look.

Useless to look with your own eyes, perhaps . . .

Celie turned in the opposite direction as the footman ran off, but her father caught her sleeve.

"Where do you think you're going, miss?"

"I want to check on Rufus," she said.

Her father gave her a stern look, but Celie gazed back without blinking. When he nodded and let go of her sleeve, she took off at a trot. But instead of going into her bedchamber, and from there into the griffins' exercise tower, she kept going down the corridor, past her rooms, and Rolf's, and Lilah's, and Bran's, until she came to a narrow staircase.

She went up the staircase and turned, and then up another staircase, to the Spyglass Tower.

The Castle had given the Spyglass Tower to Celie, Lilah, and Rolf as a refuge during the awful time when Prince Khelsh had tried to take it over. Even now that Khelsh was long gone, eaten by Rufus's father, few people but Celie ever bothered to visit it, and the maids never cleaned there.

With the Castle whole, it didn't move things around as much as it once had. Celie wasn't sure if it was because the Castle was content, or if it had less room to maneuver. Either way, the Spyglass Tower was one of the few rooms that still shifted its location, but Celie could always find it without too much effort.

Celie picked the western spyglass, which looked out over the roofs of the Castle. The spyglasses could see much farther than any normal spyglasses, looking for miles to the edges of the valley that held the Castle. They could also look through the walls of the Castle and show you what was happening inside. She took hold of the brass tube, closed her left eye, and asked the Castle to show her Wizard Arkwright.

"I can't believe we didn't think of this before," she muttered, pressing her right eye to the lens.

But there was nothing there. The view through the spyglass was of the stone walls of the Castle, the tile roofs, and nothing else. It blurred and came into focus several times as though looking for the missing wizard, but there was nothing to see.

"What does that mean?" Celie said in frustration. "Is he *not* in the Castle?"

She swung the spyglass around on its stand, scanning the village and the road out of the valley. But the lenses never focused. The road was just a gray stripe, and the village was full of brown and gray blobs, with smaller people-shaped blobs moving among them.

She studied the walls of the Castle again, but still nothing came into focus. Was Arkwright too far away for the Castle to see? Or had he used magic to hide himself? Or would the Castle have hidden him, if he asked? His family had owned the Castle at one time, after a long battle with the Hathelockes that lasted for centuries. But they had wanted the Castle and the griffins, and in the end they had tried to kill everyone in their entire world in order to possess those two things. Would the Castle feel any loyalty to Arkwright? Or had he done something to make it hide him?

"Castle?" Celie pulled back from the spyglass and put one hand on the stones of the window frame. "Are you hiding Arkwright?"

There was no answer.

Chapter
9

Hold still, Celie!"

"Why do I have to do this, Lilah? I have plenty of new gowns!"

"You keep growing!"

"It's not my fault!"

"Hold still!"

"Princess Delilah, it's *you* who are not helping," the head seamstress said.

She was on her knees beside Celie, who was standing as still as she could with her arms outstretched while the seamstress pinned the hem of her newest gown. Every time Celie moved so much as an eyebrow, Lilah scolded her. But at the seamstress's words, Lilah turned in a huff and started shuffling through the patterns on the table.

Celie dared to tilt her chin down and look at the head seamstress. The woman winked at her.

"I quite liked my *old* new gowns," Celie said. "Is it possible to just alter some of them?"

"Very possible, Your Highness," the head seamstress said. "Send them down and we'll remake them."

"Maybe the green one?" Celie asked. "I really like that one. If you could make the hem and sleeves longer, it would be wonderful."

"I'm sure we could," the head seamstress said, nodding. "That was a very nice gown, as I recall. The embroidery on the bodice was particularly fine."

"That's my favorite bit," Celie agreed.

"Absolutely not!" Lilah whirled, looking horrified. "Embroidered bodices aren't the fashion anymore! Now everything is very simple, with wider sleeves!"

"Lilah," Celie began, wincing at the hurt expression on the head seamstress's face. "I think they're very nice—"

"But they're not in *fashion*," Lilah said again. "Do you want to look frumpy in front of Lulath's family?"

Celie was going to protest that she didn't care what she looked like in front of Lulath's family, but she stopped. Lilah cared. And this was all for Lilah. Lilah was terrified that she would embarrass herself in front of Lulath's family, or that they would think she was ugly or frumpy or foolish. Queen Celina had explained all this to Celie again that morning as she'd walked her to the seamstresses' rooms like a jailer, making sure that Celie didn't run off to help Bran look for Arkwright, or check on Maisy. The maid still had not awoken, and Bran could not figure out what spell had been used to put her to sleep.

"Do you?"

With a jolt, Celie realized that Lilah was waiting for an answer.

"No, no, I don't," she muttered.

"Speak clearly, don't mumble," Lilah said.

"Oh, look, Your Highness! I found that lace you were asking about!" One of the younger seamstresses came to Celie's rescue.

"Put your shoulders back," the head seamstress said to Celie.

Celie did, tilting her chin up in the process. Over one of the cutting tables she could see the trapdoor in the ceiling. She'd come through that door and fallen on the table almost two years ago, running away from Khelsh. She thought for a chilling moment how she would probably be dead if she didn't know all the ins and outs of the Castle, the trapdoors and passageways. That was why Celie had been the first person to truly map out the Castle: she'd been the first person in centuries to explore every single secret passage and hidden door.

"Oh," Celie said. "Oh, oh, oh!"

"Did I poke you, Your Highness?" The head seamstress sat back on her heels, concerned.

"I need to get out of this gown," Celie said. "I need to find Bran."

"Don't you dare sneak off," Lilah said. "It was hard enough to track you down today!"

"Lilah," Celie said. "This is very important. More important than new gowns."

"Right now there's nothing as important as these gowns," Lilah said. Then she flushed. "I know that sounds shallow, but it's true! We have to have new wardrobes on time!"

"Lilah," Celie began, "I really, really have to talk to Bran."

"I'm all done, Your Highness," the head seamstress said. "So you can go now. We have all your measurements, and this will be hemmed today."

"Oh, good," Celie said. "Can someone get me out of this? *Now?*"

One of the other seamstresses helped Celie out of the gown, which had been pinned together in the back since the laces were not yet done. Celie was so anxious to talk to Bran that she started to run out of the sewing room in her shift, and only Lilah's scandalized cry stopped her. She hopped into her old gown, nearly ripping one of the sleeves as she jammed her arm in, and the seamstress helping her yanked the laces so tight, she could hardly breathe.

"There you are, Princess," the woman said, breathless herself at Celie's urgency. "You're ready."

Celie gave her a grateful look and took off at a run for Bran's rooms, but they were empty. She headed to her own room, to see if he was in the griffins' tower helping Pogue with Arrow, but she found herself at the front doors of the Castle instead. She turned around to go back to her room, but then there was that familiar twist in her head.

Once again she was facing the front doors.

"Can I help you, Your Highness?" The guard at the doors was staring at her.

"I'm looking for Wizard Bran," Celie said.

"He's out in the sheep meadow," the guard said. "Setting up the workshop."

"The workshop?"

"For the ship," the guard said, his eyes shining. "It's going to be an amazing sight, isn't it? A great ship, in our sheep meadow!"

"Blast Lilah and her new wardrobe," Celie snarled, startling the guard.

She pushed through the doors, muttering all the while, and went across the front courtyard and out the gate. She'd been so busy being fitted for stupid gowns, never mind learning Grathian customs from her tutor, that she'd completely forgotten about the ship, and her figurehead that was going to be used on it.

In order to use as many tools and materials as the Castle could provide, the king had decided to cut and shape the pieces of the ship in the sheep meadow, with

Bran supervising. The materials would then be moved on massive carts, which Bran also seemed to think he could build, to the Grathian docks. As part of the celebration of Lilah and Lulath's betrothal, the assembled ship would be launched in front of the Grathian court. Also attending would be Queen Celina, Celie, Rolf, and of course Lilah, all presumably in fashionable new clothes that wouldn't embarrass the Glower family.

The sheep were standing in a huddle, looking stunned. They often looked stunned, because they were sheep, but this time Celie had to agree with them. In the middle of the smooth, green meadow just to the east of the Castle, a massive structure was being erected. It was a rough shed, hardly more than a roof with support timbers, to keep the weather off the pieces of the ship, but still it was huge.

And being built incredibly fast.

"The griffins can build roofs?" Celie couldn't believe it.

The entire griffin flock was in the meadow, including Rufus and the normally fastidious Juliet, and they were helping the workers to build the shed. They carried lumber in their claws, flying it up to the top of the structure where the workers were perched. As Celie watched, mouth open, Rufus snatched up a bundle of shingles and flew them to a shirtless man straddling the center roof beam, who held out his arms to take them.

The man looked familiar.

"Is that *Pogue?*" Celie asked the sheep, but they only bleated in confusion.

Celie saw that Pogue was still as muscular as he'd been when he'd worked his father's forge every day, before he'd become Bran's assistant. She blushed and looked away. But then she saw something that only made her gape more. Dangling below Pogue was a large basket, and peering over the edge of the basket was Arrow, his sleek brown-gold head cocked in curiosity.

"Is that safe?" Celie asked the sheep once again.

"He cries if Pogue leaves him on the ground," Bran answered her.

"Oh!" Celie jumped. "Don't sneak up like that!"

"I didn't sneak," Bran said. "You were staring." He nodded to a gaggle of village girls standing to one side, their faces tilted up to watch Pogue like a field of daisies following the sun. "You might want to be less obvious, if you don't want to be lumped in with them."

Celie's cheeks turned so hot, she thought they would glow. "I was looking for *you*," she said reproachfully. "And then I saw Arrow and got worried.

"No one told me you were already building the ship," she added plaintively.

"We're not, actually, this is just the shed," Bran said.

"Still," Celie said. "I would have liked to know."

"I'm sorry," Bran said. "I was going to tell you when we started on the ship. So far we're only using lumber from our own forests, none of the things from the Castle."

Celie was mollified by the apology in his voice. "All right," she said. Then she remembered the reason she'd come running to the sheep meadow.

"Arkwright's still in the Castle," she blurted out.

"What?" Bran turned away from watching Lord and Lady Griffin, wings beating in unison, carry an enormous beam to the top of the shed. "No! We've searched, asked the Castle, and then searched again." Bran shook his head. "I don't know what happened to Maisy, or how he's getting in to steal the food and blankets, but he's not here now."

"He's in the passageways," Celie insisted.

"How could he be in the passageways?" Bran said. "There are guards patrolling them now. Maids and footmen going up and down, not to mention—"

"The *secret* passageways!" She tried to keep from raising her voice, and mostly succeeded.

Rufus heard her, though, and flew to her. He squawked happily and butted her with his head, wanting to be petted and praised for his work. Celie petted him, but her words were for Bran.

"I know he's there," she said.

"The secret passageways," Bran said slowly. "It's true, I haven't looked there.

"But there are no rooms, and the passageways are very narrow." He looked thoughtful for a moment, but then he shook his head. "I can't believe the Castle would hide Arkwright. It hates him too much for what he's done."

Bran was certainly right about that, as Celie knew only too well.

Centuries before, Arkwright had helped his uncle split the Castle's Eye into two pieces, effectively crippling the powerful Castle. Half of the Eye and half of the Castle had been sent to Sleyne with Arkwright, who had proceeded to destroy any history of the Castle or the griffin riders who had once lived in it. Half of the Castle had remained in its original home, where the Hathelocke and Arkish people had fought over it so ferociously and so long that they'd nearly all died in the battle. Celie, Rolf, Lilah, Lulath, and Pogue had managed to find and replace the other half of the Eye, and now the Castle was whole, but it was still angry at Arkwright, which made it seem ludicrous that he might find any corner of the Castle in which he could hide.

"But he's not *in* the Castle," Celie said.

"You just said——"

"He's in the *secret passageways*," Celie said, cutting him off.

"I don't understand." Bran's dark eyebrows were deeply furrowed.

"Well, you see, Bran," Rolf said, walking up with his tunic over one shoulder. "Some of us enjoy being ogled by pretty girls. Though Pogue is making the competition steep for the rest of us, and my thumbs might be broken." He wiggled his bruised-looking digits at Celie. "I was clearly not meant to be a carpenter."

"That's not what we're talking about," Celie said, still watching Bran to see if he caught on.

"Thank heavens," Rolf said. "I thought your time had come," he added in ominous tones.

"What?" Celie turned her attention to Rolf at last. "What are you talking about?"

"Yes, what?" Bran frowned even harder, making Rolf wilt a little.

"You know, Cel," he said, refusing to be totally suppressed. "I told you one day you'd look at Pogue Parry and think: now there is the finest specimen of young manhood I've ever seen! And you gagged . . . but I thought maybe you were old enough to . . . I'm sorry, did I just interrupt something horrible and serious?" He looked anxiously from Celie to Bran and back again. "What's happened?"

"Celie?" Bran said.

"The passageways weren't built by the Builder," Celie said. "They're shaped wrong. They're low and narrow. Some of the stone is different, and they never change."

Bran's face went completely white. "They're Arkish," he breathed.

"I think they added them when they were trying to take over the Castle," Celie said, grabbing his sleeve to stress her point. "To sneak around—maybe that's how they attacked the Hathelockes!"

"Fish guts," Rolf said succinctly. "If they're Arkish, then Arkwright could be hiding right next to Mother and Father's *bedchamber*."

Celie had a sudden memory of sitting in the solar with her mother and Lilah and hearing scratching at the walls. What if it hadn't been mice? What if it had been Arkwright listening to them? She grabbed at Bran's arm.

"He's in the walls," she said with terrible certainty.

"Put your shirt on and tell Sergeant Avery to meet me in the front hall," Bran told Rolf. He settled Celie's hand into the crook of his arm, pinning it there with his free hand as he hurried toward the Castle. Celie had to trot to keep up, and Rufus screeched in outrage at this treatment of his person. "And you're coming with me," Bran said to her. "The last thing we need is for you to go in there alone and get trapped in a secret passageway by Arkwright!"

"I won't be alone," Celie protested, shaking free of his grip. She was nearly running to keep up with her long-legged brother. "I'll take Rufus with me!"

Chapter
10

"Are we ready?" Bran asked. There was a blue ball of light hovering over his shoulder and he was holding a sword, which Celie didn't even know he owned.

Gathered in the front hall, nodding tensely at Bran's question, were a dozen guards, Sergeant Avery, Rolf, and King Glower. They were all well armed, standing in groups of three. Each group had a wizard light with them, to illuminate the dark passages that ran between the main rooms of the Castle. Celie was standing to one side with her mother and sister, trying not to feel put out that she'd been told in no uncertain terms that she was not to join the search.

"I fit in the passages better than half those guards," she said under her breath.

"How will they even raise their sword arms?" her mother agreed, much to her surprise. "This seems like a poor idea."

"What should we do?" Lilah fretted. "Imagine if that man has been spying on us! He could be anywhere in the Castle!" She knotted her fingers together, the knuckles showing white. "One of the passageways runs past my bedchamber," she added in a near whisper.

Celie's stomach plummeted. There was a trapdoor inside her very own room! It led down to the sewing room, and seeing it that morning had given her the idea that Arkwright might be hiding in the Castle walls. Bran hadn't assigned anyone to check the trapdoor. Celie took a single step back, easing toward the corridor that led to her bedchamber.

"Don't you dare," her mother whispered. "I know about the hatch in your floor."

"How do you—"

"That used to be *my* room when I was a girl," her mother said. "I had a deal with the seamstresses: they wouldn't tell anyone when I sneaked off, and I would bring them cake."

"That's so . . . Celie-like," Lilah said.

"Hey!" Celie said, not sure if her sister had meant it as a compliment. "It's just a trapdoor," she went on. "There's no tunnel. There's nowhere for him to hide. I just want to lock it."

"That's an excellent idea," Queen Celina said. "But come with me. I have a special lock for you to use."

The queen waved to the assembled guards. "Good luck to you all! Thank you for your service!" She swooped by King Glower and kissed his cheek. "Be careful," she admonished him in a low voice. Then she continued on toward her solar, with Celie and Lilah at her heels.

In the days since Celie had last been in her mother's solar, things had changed. The embroidery frames were gone, and there was a long table beneath the tall windows. The table held books, but also glass jars and some strange implements that looked like they'd come from Bran's rooms.

"Mother," Lilah gasped. "What have you been doing?"

"A little of this and that," the queen said airily.

"Does Bran know?"

"Lilah," their mother said. "I hardly need my own son's permission to study magic! Both my parents were wizards, you know!"

"They were?" Celie dropped the brass mallet she'd picked up with a clatter. "Grandmother, too?"

"Yes, did you not know that?" Queen Celina looked at Celie in surprise.

Celie shook her head.

"My mother was a highly respected wizard," the queen said, and her face grew sad. "She died when I was so young. I suppose I haven't shared many memories with you because I have so few."

"I knew she was a wizard," Lilah said. "And that's why I don't like this." She gestured to the table. "Put that down, Celie!"

Celie dropped the mallet again.

"Bran told me that Grandmother got into terrible trouble playing with magic," Lilah said. "If you want to learn, you need to go the College of Wizardry and get proper instruction!"

"My mother went to the College of Wizardry," Queen Celina said in the coldest voice Celie had ever heard her mother use with her children. Lilah took a step back. "And yet she still died . . . not *playing* with magic, but doing something that she cared about deeply.

"Spells go wrong," their mother said after a long, uncomfortable pause. "Anyone with an ounce of magic knows and understands that, Delilah." She drew a deep breath. "I am being careful, and I don't need you to tell tales on me. This is important, and I know I have enough skill to handle this." She held up a brass box with a knob on one side.

"What is it?" Celie asked.

"It's a lock," her mother said, her voice warming as she turned the contraption over in her hands, showing them all the sides. "A special kind of lock. If you put this on the trapdoor in your room, Celie, and turn the knob, it will lock it forever."

"Forever? You can change the Castle forever?" Celie stared at the lock.

"I think so," the queen said. "That is, if you're right, and the trapdoor is something put in later, by the Arkish. I was working on a way to keep the griffins in the stable, should we need to confine them. I can get it to work on things like trunks and wardrobes, but it doesn't work on any of the Castle doors."

"Is the Castle too powerful?"

Her mother nodded. "Yes, it seems to be. And also, the Hathelocke magic that created the Castle is very different from the kind of magic I'm used to.

"I have a suspicion, since Arkwright was able to hide himself among the College wizards for so long, that Arkish magic is very similar to what we know."

"So it might work on his magic?"

"Yes, exactly!"

"Maybe," Lilah said, slowly stepping up to the table, "it's not that Arkish magic is like College magic. Maybe it's that the College of Wizardry learned their magic from Arkwright."

"What?" Queen Celina gaped at her older daughter.

"The College was founded *four* hundred years ago," Lilah said. "And Arkwright came to Sleyne with the Castle *five* hundred years ago, and has apparently worked with the College since the day it opened."

"I never—it's true that he—" the queen stammered. "Good grief. The magic in our world may have been created by that evil man!"

"Lilah, I think Bran was right," Celie said after a moment of shock. "You do have a brain under all that hair."

"Thank you," Lilah said with asperity. "Now, can we be sure that these locks won't explode or turn us all green?"

"It won't explode," Queen Celina said softly.

Lilah put her hand to her mouth. "I'm sorry," she said.

Celie had seen her mother flinch when Lilah said "explode," and now her mother's face looked lined with pain. What had happened to her grandmother? No one ever talked about her. All Celie had ever heard was that she had died tragically when the queen was just a child.

"Do you . . . should we try it?" Celie asked, not sure she wanted to break into the mood that was filling the room.

"Yes, let's," the queen said, shaking herself a little and smiling at Celie. "It can't hurt . . . I promise."

Lady Griffin roused herself from the space beneath the table where she had been sleeping, and stretched luxuriously as they gathered up the lock and a few other things Celie's mother said they might need. The queen of the griffins rubbed her head against the queen of Sleyne, and followed them out of the room.

"Has she bonded with you?" Lilah asked as they crossed the now-empty main hall to Celie's rooms.

"In her own way, I suppose," Queen Celina said, stroking the golden head bobbing beside her. "We're not as close as you and Juliet, or Celie and Rufus, but it's been an unexpected blessing."

"She looks good," Celie said. "Fat and happy."

"Perhaps a bit *too* fat and happy," Queen Celina said. "I hope I haven't been spoiling her. Or perhaps the extra padding around her middle is more natural, now that they're safe and have plenty of food."

Once they were in Celie's room, they had to move the old sofa that was over the trapdoor. Its clawed feet scraped loudly across the floor and Celie winced, but she doubted anyone but the three of them heard. They were all busy using her idea to search the passageways for Arkwright.

"Now let's see what we've got here," Queen Celina said.

She handed Celie the lock. Celie took it with careful hands, still worried about something exploding. It was surprisingly light. The queen knelt beside the wooden square in the floor of Celie's bedchamber. It had a simple iron latch that was set into an indentation in the door so that a carpet could be laid flat over it. The queen turned the latch and Celie held her breath as her mother opened the door.

All three of them peered through the hole in the floor.

"Can I help you, Your Majesty?" The head seamstress stared up at them, a needle poised in one hand and the skirt of Celie's new gown in the other. Her eyes were wide. The other seamstresses all let out little shrieks of surprise.

"No, I'm sorry," Queen Celina called down cheerfully. "We are going to lock this trapdoor for good, and I just thought I would check it first."

"Very well, Your Majesty," said the head seamstress, completely unfazed.

"I didn't know that was there," one of the other women said. "How did I not know that was there?"

"Too much time looking down, not enough looking up," the head seamstress said. "Which is surprising, considering how much time you waste when you should be sewing!"

The younger woman looked down at her work, cheeks reddening.

"Carry on, Your Majesty," the head seamstress said.

"Thank you," Queen Celina said.

They closed the trapdoor and Celie's mother nodded to her. Celie gingerly set the lock over the latch. Queen Celina nodded again, and Celie turned the knob.

Nothing happened.

Then there was a click, and the trapdoor raised up a little. Celie sat back on her heels.

"Is that right?" she said, her voice little more than a whisper.

"I think so," Queen Celina replied. She reached out to touch the lock.

The whole trapdoor moved.

"It's not attached to the floor anymore," Lilah said in surprise. "Is that supposed to happen?"

They all scooted back and then the queen tried to lift the lock off the wooden door, but the whole door came with it. The queen dropped it with a whoosh of breath.

"Heavy," she remarked, then frowned.

"It's gone!" Celie said.

"What do you mean?" Queen Celina prodded the lock again. It was still firmly attached to the trapdoor.

"Lift it up," Celie said. "The whole thing! There's nothing underneath!"

Her mother took hold of the lock, and Celie grabbed the hinges of the trapdoor and they raised it up. Underneath, there was only a smooth stone floor, with no sign of any opening. There wasn't even a mark to show where the door had once attached to the floor.

"Was it supposed to do that?" Lilah said.

"Well, it's certainly one way to close a door for good," Queen Celina replied.

Chapter 11

—❧—

Bran had sent out five groups of men to search the passageways for Wizard Arkwright, and by midnight, only four of them had returned. None of the four groups had found Arkwright, or seen any sign that he was hiding in the walls, which was discouraging to say the least. But discouragement turned to anxiety as the hours passed and the fifth group still had not returned.

Especially since the fifth group was the one led by King Glower.

"Bran, you've got to find him," Queen Celina said in a low voice.

The family, minus King Glower, was standing just below the dais in the throne room. Lulath had gone to put his girls and Lorcan to bed, and Pogue had come in from the sheep meadow. He was armed with a handful of oatcakes to keep Arrow busy while they talked, and kept nervously taking bites out of the stale things himself.

"Which direction did they go?" Queen Celina asked.

"They were headed toward the lower levels," Bran said, also speaking quietly so that those gathered in the throne room around them couldn't hear. "The laundry, sewing room, pantries."

"Right where *he's* dared to steal food and blankets," Queen Celina said, and Celie saw her mother's eyes flutter closed for an instant. Bran started to say something, but she held up one hand. "Don't tell me: your father insisted."

"He did," Bran confirmed. "I was torn between going there, and searching the passageways that run behind the Heart of the Castle and the throne room." He looked pale and tense. "There are twice as many passages as there were before." He cut his eyes at Celie and then said, "We gave each group a copy of Celie's atlas . . . but I'm sorry, Cel, the passages weren't there, so . . ."

"I'm the one who should be apologizing," Celie said, feeling awful. "If I'd spent more time fixing the atlas after we got back—"

"It's not your fault, Celie darling," the queen said, almost angrily. "It's because the Castle is twice as large!

"I wish Owen had listened to me," she went on. "I wanted to find another way!"

"If Arkwright *is* hidden in the walls," Bran said, sounding defensive, "he could have heard us plotting. We needed to strike quickly."

"I know," Queen Celina said. "But it doesn't make this situation any less upsetting—we've got to find your father and the men with him as quickly as may be." She pressed her hands to her cheeks and then dropped them, smoothing her skirts so that no one would see how nervous she was. "And after that . . . Bran, if what you told me is true . . . we have to find Arkwright at once. We can't wait for the College to help. We have to take care of him. Now."

"I know that," Bran said, his voice rising. People turned to look at them, and Bran scowled, ducking his head.

"What is it?" Celie asked. "What did Bran tell you?"

"It's nothing," Bran said.

"It isn't nothing, or you would tell me," Celie argued, frustrated. "Stop trying to keep secrets!"

"Bran, she has a point," Queen Celina said. "None of us would be here if it weren't for her." She made a small gesture to gather Lilah, Lulath, and Pogue closer as well.

"Arkwright had plans—big plans," Bran explained. "That's why I locked him up and sent for someone from the College to collect him. It's not just because of what he had done, but what he wanted to do."

"Which is what?" Lilah's eyes were enormous.

"He assumed that one day his uncle would send for him, and that he would return to Hatheland," Bran said in a low voice. "They would finally raise an army of griffins, and take control of the Castle, and rule over their land like they had planned. When you all brought the Castle here, and the last of the griffins, he knew he'd never return." Bran sighed and rubbed his face. "So he thought he'd just have to rule here. He told me that he and he alone truly understood the Castle, and the griffins, and that he'd share that with me if I let him free and helped him . . . depose Father."

"You mean kill him?" Lilah said.

"He didn't actually say that, but it was definitely implied," Bran said, swallowing thickly. "Of course I refused. Even if he hadn't wanted me to murder my own father, this is *our* Castle, *our* country, these are *our* griffins now, and I wasn't going to betray any of that."

Queen Celina squeezed his arm.

"He escaped the next day," Bran said. "When I couldn't find him in the Castle, I reckoned that he'd fled, possibly to cause trouble, possibly just to hide from me." His eyes flashed. "I made my thoughts about his plot to rule Sleyne very clear."

"He wants us all dead, and himself wearing the crown," Pogue said in horror.

"The crown that Daddy is wearing *right now*," Celie said, and didn't bother to keep her voice down.

On the dais beside the throne, Lord Griffin raised his head and looked over. At his side, Lady Griffin continued to doze, blissfully unaware of what was happening. But her mate carefully rose and stepped away from her. He looked at the throne, and then paced around it, as though he, too, wondered where the king might be.

"We can track Daddy," Celie said, a light dawning.

"What?" Bran looked down at her, and his face cleared. "Yes, I have all the things in my room! Pogue, I'll need you to help me. Mother, could you bring me something of Father's to use? Perhaps his nightshirt—"

"We don't need all that," Celie said, interrupting. "We only need him."

She pointed to Lord Griffin, standing at attention next to the throne.

"You think he can track Father?" Bran looked skeptical. "Rufus could track you, I'm sure. But I don't know how deep the bond goes between him and Father."

Pogue looked up from feeding Arrow. "It's deep enough, I think," he said. "And well worth a try. At least while you put together your spell. That one is king of the griffins with good reason."

Bran paused for a moment before he nodded. "It's worth a try."

"I'll do it," Celie offered. "You can get your spell ready if you want."

"Come on, you," Pogue said to Arrow as he followed Celie. "I'll go with her," he told Bran. He raised his voice and called out, "Sergeant Avery, we need you."

Now all eyes were on Celie and her family, and she felt a prickle of nerves. She approached Lord Griffin and gave a little curtsy. The griffin stared at her.

"Sir, we need to find my father," Celie said. "Can you help us? Can you help us find the king?" She mimed putting a crown on her own head.

She was never sure how much the griffins understood. The entire court had been speculating on this since the griffins had arrived. It might be sheer coincidence when they did something that someone asked them to do. Yet it seemed equally possible that they understood Sleynth perfectly, but chose not to pay attention most of the time.

Whether it was coincidence or true understanding, Celie didn't know. But the king of the griffins screeched and leaped down from the dais. He paced twice in front of Celie, scenting the air, and then he walked out of the throne room. Celie, Pogue, and Sergeant Avery followed. As they passed Avery's men, he signaled for three of them to follow, and they went out into the main hall.

Lord Griffin led them down the corridor toward the kitchens, but he stopped before he reached them. He sniffed for a moment and continued on. Then he stopped and scratched at the door of one of the cupboards that lined the corridor.

"Is that the entrance to a passage?" Pogue whispered.

"If it is, it's not one I know about," Celie admitted. She resisted the urge to find pencils and paper and make notes. She needed to find her father first.

They opened the cupboard, but it was full of towels. The guardsmen lifted them out and stacked them neatly to one side, and Pogue knocked on the back wall of the cupboard.

"It sounds solid," he told Celie. "Do you know how to open these things?"

"There should be a latch," Celie said.

But no matter how she looked, she couldn't see one. She ducked under the shelf that was just at the height of her chin, feeling every inch of the wooden paneling for a latch or a knot or something that would indicate an opening. She looked to Lord Griffin, but he was preening his wings, apparently done with guiding them. Celie pressed against the back of the cupboard with both hands, trying to see if the wood would give even a little.

There was a click and the back of the cupboard swung back into darkness.

"Very nice," Pogue said. "Let's move these."

He pulled one of the shelves out and the guardsmen got the others. They stacked the shelves to one side and then stood back, waiting for Celie to lead.

"Your wings are spotless and you know it," she said to Lord Griffin, who was still fussing over his feathers. "We need you to lead us to my father. Please."

The griffin stared at her for a moment, but she refused to look away. Griffins were proud, and they were frightening and wonderful at the same time, but Celie was a princess, and she was not going to let anyone boss her around. Not even the king of the griffins.

After a long moment he bobbed his head and went into the passageway ahead of them. Celie made to follow, but there was a scream from down the corridor, and Rufus came barreling toward them, wings half-raised. Celie held up a hand to stop him, and he slid to a halt right in front of her. He made angry noises, as though upset that she was leaving him behind, or maybe demanding that she not go into the dark tunnel—she wasn't sure.

But Lord Griffin turned around and silenced Rufus with a single sharp squawk of command. Rufus didn't leave, however, and stared back at his father until Lord Griffin gave what Celie could only describe as a griffin shrug. The griffin king turned and proceeded down the dark passageway, and Celie and Rufus followed him. After a moment, Celie had to shove Rufus behind her, because the passages weren't wide enough for them to walk side by side. Rufus yelped and Pogue apologized for stepping on his tail, and they stumbled on in the dark.

"Princess," one of the men from the back called. "We're losing the light from the doorway . . . can we light a lamp?"

"Oh, sorry," Celie said.

Lord Griffin hadn't stopped, and she didn't want him to get too far ahead, so she felt along the wall as they kept walking. There were little stone ledges that held lamps and tinderboxes scattered throughout the passages.

There was a crack, and Pogue swore.

"Found a lamp," he groaned.

"You're not supposed to find it with your face," one of the guards said, laughing. Then he made an *oof* noise like he'd been jabbed in the stomach and added, "My apologies, Sir Pogue."

Pogue grunted a reply and lit the lamp as they walked, no mean feat, for Lord Griffin was keeping a brisk pace, as though he knew precisely where they were going. Pogue held the lamp high once it was lit, though there was really nothing to see but the endless stone passageway. There were cross passages, but the griffin king never turned. As far as Celie could tell, they were running along the back of the Castle, in the newer part that had just arrived. That meant that they were probably the first people who had walked that passageway for centuries.

Pogue had that thought at the same time as Celie.

"You'd think it would be dusty, or full of spiders," he said.

"Spiders," Sergeant Avery said. "Why? Were there a lot of spiders in that place?"

"Sergeant," Pogue said, laughing, "don't tell me you're afraid of spiders!"

"You can't use a sword against a spider," Sergeant Avery said, defensive.

"In the jungles of Bendeswe, they have spiders large enough to prey on the jungle wildcats," Pogue said.

"Now, why in the name of all that's holy would you tell me that?" Sergeant Avery said. "I could have lived a long and happy life without ever knowing that!"

"So could I," Celie said fervently.

"Aw, Sergeant," one of the guards said. "Now we know your weakness!" He laughed, but then Celie hissed and the man cut off abruptly.

Lord Griffin had stopped.

"What is it?" Pogue whispered.

Celie didn't know, but the griffin king was highly alert. His wings were half-raised and the feathers around his neck were bristled. He was staring into the cross passage with unsettling intensity.

"What is it?" Celie whispered to him.

Rufus whined and butted her in the back with his head, trying to get her to move.

"Celie," Pogue whispered. "I'm going to slide around you and Rufus."

"And I'm right behind him," Sergeant Avery said, and Celie heard the rasp of his sword being drawn. "Press yourself against the wall, Your Highness."

Celie didn't argue. The lamp cast almost no light into the cross passage, and she was suddenly aware of how vulnerable she and Rufus were, there at the front of the line in this narrow passage. If Lord Griffin didn't step forward into the intersection more, they wouldn't have any room to fight. But he wouldn't move, he just stood.

Right as Pogue moved past Celie, Lord Griffin opened his beak and screamed a war cry. Pogue froze and Celie let out a much smaller scream of her own.

"All right?" Pogue asked as the sound died away.

"Yes, but you're on my foot," she said, pain shooting through her toes.

"Sorry!" Pogue stepped back as much as he could.

Then Lord Griffin moved, and Pogue followed him into the cross passage. Sergeant Avery was right behind him, squeezing past Celie with a muttered apology. Celie stepped out behind the sergeant, however, not letting his men get in her way. She had a sudden premonition of what they would find around the corner.

"Your Majesty!" Pogue cried.

Celie rounded the corner and saw that she was right, and she was both relieved and angry. Her father, King Glower, and his men were trussed up and stacked against the wall like luggage.

Chapter 12

I can't wake him," Bran said, back in the throne room.
"I can't wake any of them." He was visibly shaking. "I
don't even know why he bothered to tie them up." He ran
a trembling hand over his face. "I can't wake them."

The court had been dismissed and it was only the
Glower family, Lulath, Pogue, and Sergeant Avery. The
king and the men who had been with him were lying on
cots in the Heart of the Castle, with Sergeant Avery's
best men to guard them. Maisy, the little maid who had
also been stricken down by Arkwright's spell, had been
brought to join them so that Bran could study them all
at once.

"You need time," Queen Celina said. "No one expects
you to cure them immediately."

"But . . . it's *Father*." Bran's voice cracked.

"You can do this, Bran," Queen Celina said firmly.

"I don't want to be Glower the Eightieth again," Rolf said, ashen faced.

"You won't be," the queen told him, putting one arm around her younger son and giving him a little squeeze. "I will be the acting regent while your father is . . . unwell."

"What are your orders, my queen?" Sergeant Avery was clearly uncomfortable just standing there, when the king was under a spell and there was a wicked wizard loose in the walls and both the Royal Wizard and the Crown Prince were almost in tears.

Celie could appreciate that, as well. She didn't want to stand there one more minute. She wanted to go, to fight, to do something. She wanted to shake her father awake, and run Arkwright through with a sword. She also wanted to hide in her room and cry, or go flying on Rufus to let the wind dry her tears and carry away the sound of her sobs.

Queen Celina drew a deep breath, thinking. Her eyes closed for a moment.

"He's like a rat," offered Pogue, interrupting the queen's meditation and turning all eyes to him. "We need to treat him like one, and flush him out of the walls before he causes more damage. Your Majesty."

"How do you propose we do that?" Queen Celina asked.

"The guards marked the walls of the passages they checked," Pogue said. "And that's a good start. We need to make sure everyone knows them, though, and understands the code. We need to look for any signs that he uses those passages, or sleeps in them."

The queen nodded. "And I have my lock," she said.

"What's this?" Bran recovered himself, squinting at his mother.

"Oh, yes, it's so clever," Celie said. "We used it today—yesterday, I mean. It was amazing!"

"We locked the trapdoor in Celie's bedroom," Lilah put in. "And now it's just . . . gone! Poof! I couldn't believe it!"

"Poof?" Bran was frowning now. "Mother . . . you're not dabbling, are you? Is that wise?"

"Bran," the queen said. "I don't appreciate the term 'dabbling', and I'm not going to discuss the wisdom of my actions here." She eyed Sergeant Avery, who found something fascinating to stare at on his own boots. "The point is that I have a way of getting rid of the doors and passages in this Castle!"

"But what if this goes wrong?" Bran argued. "It worked the first time, yes, but . . ." He gave her a meaningful look.

No one knew what to say for a moment, and then Pogue broke the silence by clearing his throat.

"Am I the only one who is upset about the fact that Celie had a trapdoor in her bedroom?" he asked. "I mean, not that it's my place to be upset . . . but . . . how long has that been there?"

"All my life," Celie said, shrugging. "It goes directly into the sewing room below." Then she corrected herself. "It *went* into the sewing room, that is. It's gone now."

"It was there when I was a child, too," Queen Celina said. "That used to be my room."

"And it's gone?" Bran looked like he was struggling with several emotions at once. "Just not there? Or doesn't open anymore?"

"It's gone," Celie said. "The door is just leaning against the wall now, and it's smooth stone underneath. And in the sewing room, there's just ceiling, no more wooden hatch."

"Is the hatch in good shape?" Pogue asked suddenly.

"Ye-es," Celie said. "Why?"

"Oh . . . I just thought . . . it's not important right now, but we could use it for the ship."

"Oh," Celie said. "I guess." She sighed. There was no point in protesting, she supposed. If they wanted something for the ship, they would just take it.

"All right, all right," Bran said. "I want to see this lock, but I think we're better off sending the soldiers through the walls, to mark them and look for signs of Arkwright."

"I don't like this at all," Rolf announced. "Mother, you of all people—"

"I said I don't want to discuss this right now," Queen Celina cut in. "And I meant it. It's late, and we all need to go to bed."

But first everyone insisted on filing through Celie's room and inspecting the smoothly flagged floor where the trapdoor had been. They looked at the door, stacked against the wall, and made *hmm* noises. Except for Pogue, who picked up the trapdoor and raised his eyebrows at Celie. She sighed again and closed her eyes for a moment before she nodded for him to take it.

The queen produced the brass lockbox and offered to demonstrate it, but Bran shouted, "No!"

"There is no need for that," the queen said, her voice ice cold. "We should all retire now." And she swept out without looking back.

The others shuffled out of Celie's room, looking angry or tired or upset to various degrees. Pogue was the last one out, after checking that Arrow was asleep in a basket in the griffin tower above Celie's bedchamber. As he picked up the trapdoor and started to carry it out, though, Celie caught his sleeve.

"Why is everyone so upset about Mother doing magic?" she asked. It was sometimes useful, but sometimes irritating, that people told Pogue things they wouldn't tell her.

He looked uncomfortable. "I shouldn't say, if you don't know," he said.

"Pogue," Celie said, hurt. "It isn't fair that I don't know, and you know it!"

"It's how your grandmother died," Pogue said reluctantly. "She was a wizard, you know."

"I just found that out today," she said.

"Well, they don't talk about it much," he admitted.

"Why not? I think it's amazing that Mummy's parents were both wizards!"

"Er, it's just that . . . when she died . . . ," Pogue said, hesitating.

"Yes?"

"She wasn't a wizard when she died," Pogue said in a rush. "They banned her from magic, for messing with spells that were too dangerous."

Celie felt wobbly. "They do that?" She'd never heard of such a thing.

"You, um, have to . . . do some really bad things," Pogue said. "She wasn't *evil*," he added quickly, when Celie's mouth dropped open in shock. "She just wouldn't stop doing things that, if they went wrong, could hurt people. And then she kept on, and eventually she . . . blew herself up."

"What?" Celie's knees buckled and she half fell onto a footstool.

Pogue dropped the trapdoor and knelt down by her. "Are you all right?"

"Yes," she said faintly. "I think . . .?"

"I'm so sorry I'm telling you this," he said. "But, to be honest, if the queen is going to start meddling with magic when she hasn't had any training, you ought to know why your brother is so upset."

"She blew herself up?"

"And a couple of maids who were helping her," Pogue added, looking grim.

"And they're dead?"

"Very."

"Where was this?"

"She was using one of the guest rooms at the back of the Castle for her spells," Pogue said, "since the Royal Wizard, her husband, had taken away her workshop."

"Ugh, that's so . . . I don't know what that is," Celie said.

"It's bad," Pogue said. "But that won't happen to your mother."

"It won't?"

"Your mother is too smart to do things that might . . . end that way."

"I hope so," Celie said.

Pogue squeezed her shoulder and got to his feet. "I should go."

"Thanks for telling me," Celie said.

"You're welcome, I suppose," he said. "I'm just sorry I had to be the one."

"It sounds better coming from you," Celie told him. "Daddy just blusters and sometimes Bran is just too . . . *wizardly*."

"Thank you," Pogue said. He bowed. "I try my best." Then he picked up the trapdoor again. "And, Celie?"

"Yes?"

"I'm so sorry about your father. The king. I'm sure that Bran will find a cure."

"Thank you," she said as he went out.

Celie closed and locked her door, and went upstairs to spend some time with the griffins. She had an awful lot to think about, but one thing she was sure of: She was going to get that lockbox again, and she was going to use it to get rid of Arkwright.

For her father.

Chapter
13

It was a week before Celie managed to get her hands on the lockbox, however. A week in which no one found any sign of Arkwright, and everyone became short-tempered and paranoid. No one would tell Celie anything, and even Queen Celina refused to let her younger daughter help look for the villain.

But although Queen Celina disliked being reminded of her own mother's disgrace, she also was not foolish enough to let Celie play with magic. Even Celie's arguments that since the box had worked just fine once, there was no reason they couldn't use it again had been met with flat refusal. Bran had commandeered the lockbox and hidden it somewhere in his workroom. He said that he would let them use it after he had run some tests himself, but he was busy trying to find a counterspell to wake up King Glower and the others, and wouldn't so much as look at the lockbox until that was done.

"It's more important that we wake your father," said Queen Celina.

She and Celie were standing in the sheep meadow, watching lengths of lumber be cut into planks for the ship and taking a break from sitting in the Heart of the Castle with the king, Maisy, and the stricken guards.

There were more village girls than sheep clustered on the green lawn today, because the heat had caused more of the workers than Pogue to remove their shirts. Added to that, Lorcan, Juliet, and Arrow were all playing in the field under the watchful eye of Ethan, which made the girls all coo over the baby griffins in a manner that Celie found more than a little cloying.

"But why can't we work on both?" Celie persisted. "Father *and* flushing out Arkwright?"

She watched in satisfaction as Rufus, who had just joined the sporting griffins, hissed at a girl who tried to offer him a bunch of flowers. "He doesn't eat flowers," Celie called to the girl, annoyed. She turned back to her mother. "We shouldn't just be standing here because Bran said so! There's so much to do!"

"Bran is the Royal Wizard," her mother said.

"Twice someone has tried to break into the griffin stables," Celie reminded her mother. "Arkwright wants a griffin; he's not content to wait and see if one wants to bond anymore. What if he's worked out a spell to force a griffin to do his bidding? Or put them all to sleep?"

"Oh, he couldn't possibly!" Queen Celina protested halfheartedly. "Bran says that we shouldn't use the lockbox until after he's approved it."

"What does Bran know about it? He wasn't there when we used it."

"This is a large part of his job: to suss out magical threats and defuse them," Queen Celina said gently.

"You're not a magical threat!" Celie said, shocked that her mother would even say such a thing.

Her mother smiled. "Good heavens, I should hope not. But the lockbox is," she explained. "It's an untested magical device created by someone who is not a wizard." She sounded as though she were reciting a lesson. Perhaps she was.

"Why didn't you go to the College of Wizardry?" Celie asked. "You should be a wizard!" Something occurred to her then. "If you can use magic, doesn't that mean you're a wizard anyway?"

"I didn't want to go back then," her mother explained. "I wanted to stay here, and marry your father. The Castle wanted it, too, remember?"

Celie nodded. Everyone knew the story of how Celie's father, then Crown Prince, and the daughter of the Royal Wizard had been locked in the throne room together for six hours. When at last the doors of the throne room had opened, Celie's grandfathers, also known as King Glower the Seventy-eighth and Royal Wizard Finnegan, had found their two oldest children sitting on the floor, holding hands, planning their marriage.

"Daddy would have waited for you, and I'm sure the Castle would have, too," Celie said.

"Your father needed me," she said. "And so did the Castle. Poor Rolf died not long after that, and your father was a king at barely nineteen."

"What?" Celie stared at her mother, then looked over to the building site, where she could see Rolf helping to hold a large beam.

"Oh, Rolf is named after your grandfather," Queen Celina hastily clarified. "Did you not know that? Glower the Seventy-eighth was born Rolf, just like our Rolf." Her tone was wistful, and she was also watching Rolf.

Celie remembered the sorrow she'd felt when Rolf had been crowned Glower the Eightieth the year before. After the coronation, only she and Lilah had had the right to call him Rolf, and even then people had frowned when they had. Of course, their father was restored to the throne just days later, but it had still been a strange and terrifying time.

And one day Rolf would be Glower the Eightieth again. But hopefully not very soon.

Celie wondered if she would have a son one day, and if she would name him Owen. Would she have to explain that it had been her father's name, but no one had called him that except his wife? Probably.

"Who started that?" Celie asked.

"Who started what?"

"Who started calling our kings Glower? And why Glower, and not Sleyne?" Celie asked.

"From what I can tell, it was the first king of the Castle, who I suppose was really Arkish," her mother said. "But I thought you knew that . . ."

"Yes," Celie said. "But I still don't understand why these exiles from Hatheland and the Glorious Arkower didn't try to blend in better. Shouldn't they have called it Castle Sleyne, and tried to pretend they were always from here?"

"You and I would have done that," Queen Celina said. "But they were too proud, I think. And too strange. I wonder how long it took people to really accept them, and to come to trust them, and the Castle."

"I suppose," Celie said slowly. A new thought was creeping into her brain.

Her mother saw her face change. "What is it."

"What happened to the old king of Sleyne? The one who was here when the Castle arrived."

"Ah!" Her mother beamed. "An excellent question, darling! And one that I can actually answer," she said eagerly.

Celie held up a hand to stop her, though. "Will I like the answer?" she asked.

"Yes," Queen Celina said. "I promise!"

"All right," Celie said, lowering her hand. "What is it?"

"Sleyne had no king."

"What?" Celie blinked at her mother. "How is that possible?"

"There had been a king, you see," the queen said. "But he'd died a couple of years before, of very old age. Both of his sons had died without leaving any heirs, and he had only one daughter, who died about the same time. The king was *very* old; he and his children had lived long full lives," she explained before Celie could ask. "The daughter had married a Bendeswean noble, and the Sleynth asked for one of her sons to be the new king, but none of them were interested."

Celie was outraged. "Why wouldn't they want to be king? And Sleyne is much better than Bendeswe! Aren't they always having those awful dust storms?"

"These princes had never been to Sleyne," the queen went on, laughing a little at Celie's outburst. "I don't think they even spoke Sleynth. They wanted to give Sleyne to their king so that he could make it part of Bendeswe, and he would give them large estates in return."

"They sound horrible!"

"They do," her mother agreed. "But you have to understand: Sleyne was very poor back then. The king had not been well for some time, and his Council did most of the work, but they were also old and feeble. Bendeswe and

Vhervhine had both taken large bites out of our borders, roads were in bad repair, schools were out of funds . . . Sleyne was no prize." She paused. "I suspect that's why those horrible wizards thought it would make a good place to put the Castle, when they were trying to get it away from the plague in Hatheland. They could have taken control of Sleyne without any fight. And they did, in a roundabout way."

"I think I hate Glower the First now," Celie said. "I didn't know that he just took over because the old king had been . . . old."

"Well, we shouldn't hate him," her mother said. "My understanding was that the people of Sleyne greeted the Arkish and Hathelockes like saviors. Glower the First offered to rebuild the kingdom and take back the land that had been nibbled away. Which he did, and then he even married a Sleynth noblewoman," she reminded Celie. "So he *was* trying."

"And Arkwright probably helped him," Celie said, unsure of how she felt about *that* part of the story.

"Probably," her mother agreed.

"So the history of the Castle is both good and bad?"

"Most history is," Queen Celina said.

"I suppose," Celie said.

Celie didn't really care for history, mainly because Master Humphries, her tutor, made even the bloodiest battle sound like a terribly dull affair. It had never occurred to her that each army thought they were in the right. But she supposed they did think that, just like the Arkish and Hathelocke people who had come to Sleyne thought they were doing the right thing by taking over. And had they? Sleyne wouldn't exist if they hadn't.

But if they'd never come here, there would still be unicorns frolicking in the meadow . . . and all the griffins would be dead.

"It's not the most comfortable feeling, is it, Celie darling?" Queen Celina sounded sympathetic. "When you realize that sometimes right and wrong is hard to judge?"

"No," Celie agreed. "I guess it's not."

Celie had already had to come to terms with the fact that the feasts and decorations in the holiday feasting hall were not made magically by the Castle. Instead, for hundreds of years, the people of the Glorious Arkower had made a pilgrimage to the Castle to prepare the feasts as an annual tribute to their long-lost home. Every day for a week, over the winter solstice, wonderful feasts and decorations would be laid out in the Heart of the Castle, and then the room would be transferred to Sleyne, where Celie and her family would enjoy their holiday feast, thinking the Castle had provided all, and not some mysterious people in a far-off land, who were only providing the feast as part of a half remembered tradition.

Now that the Heart of the Castle was permanently in Sleyne, the holiday feasts that year would be very different, but Celie was glad. She still felt strange twinges when she thought about the unknown hands that had prepared the old feasts. Hands that had worshipped the Castle, and the people in it, for hundreds of years without even knowing who or where they were.

Celie turned, not sure what else to say, and watched the work on the ship for a time. It looked like they were assembling a great wooden skeleton. She said this aloud, and her mother agreed.

"It's the bones of the ship," she said. "Just like the stones of the Castle are its bones, I suppose. They're using whatever lumber they can find in the Castle, you know."

Celie nodded. She did know that. There had been a whole cache of lumber in one of the new rooms, as well as the fittings from the original ship that she'd found in the storeroom with the figurehead.

"The ship will be part Hathelocke and part Sleynth," her mother said. "And a very fitting gift for Lilah and Lulath." She looked at Celie. "I know you don't like its being taken away from you. I hope you'll come to be at peace with Daddy's decision."

"I am," Celie said, and was surprised to realize that it was starting to be true.

But now, as she said it, something else bothered her. Their family wasn't just Sleynth, it was also Hathelocke and Arkish. And there were no Arkish bits to add to the ship.

"There's even a piece that's Arkish," her mother said, as though reading her thoughts.

"What? Is there?"

"Yes, Pogue told me that he's planning to use the trap-door from your room," the queen said.

"That won't be enough," Celie said, mostly to herself.

"What was that, darling?"

"Nothing," Celie said. "I need to go. I think my nose is getting sunburned."

The queen looked at her intently for a moment, then said, "Go on, then, darling." She put a soft hand on Celie's shoulder and squeezed lightly. "I'm going to go sit with your father."

Chapter
14

⟩≈⟨

Celie was at Bran's door in a matter of minutes, with Rufus on her heels. Several months ago the Castle had put most of the Glower family rooms along one corridor on the opposite side of the main hall, and there they had stayed. Bran's rooms were across the corridor and one door down from Celie's, and it would be easy for her to pretend that she was on her way to her own room if anyone should come.

Bran's door was locked.

Of course it was. He'd always been secretive, even before he became a wizard. Celie stared at the door in despair. She just had to get that lockbox!

She looked around, but Bran and Pogue were busy in the Heart of the Castle, looking up counterspells and grinding strange herbs into potions. They'd roped Rolf, Celie's tutor Master Humphries, and the more scholarly

Councilors into helping them. The guards, along with the younger and more warlike Councilors, were patrolling the passageways with Celie's atlas in hand, marking the walls with chalk. But if they found Arkwright, what could they do?

Celie had to get rid of the passageways, get rid of Arkwright, and give the ship some Arkish lumber. To make things fair.

"I have to," she said aloud. Rufus clacked his beak in agreement.

There was a twisting sensation in the back of her brain, which meant that the Castle was moving.

The door to Bran's rooms swung open.

"You're my witness," she said to Rufus. "If Bran gets mad, you saw the Castle open this door, right?"

Rufus clacked again, and butted her with his head to make her walk forward.

Bran had two private rooms: his workroom and his bedchamber. The workroom was first, and the lockbox was right in plain sight on a long table where Bran had left it amid a clutter of other wizardly things.

"Hello?" Celie called, still standing at the threshold despite Rufus's urging.

When there was no answer, she dared to step into the room. She half expected to be struck by some sort of spell to repel burglars or nosy siblings, but nothing happened. A few more steps, and she reached the table. She wiped her sweaty palms on her skirt and picked up the lockbox with shaking fingers. She hadn't been nervous about using it the first time, but that was before she'd found out about her grandmother, and before her wizard brother had taken the box for everyone's good.

Celie walked out of Bran's room as quickly as she could without actually running, which she reckoned would attract more attention if anyone saw her. She hurried along the corridor and into her own room, holding the lockbox in the folds of her skirt on the left side, the side Rufus was walking on. They didn't see anyone, though, and whisked into Celie's room without incident.

In her room, Celie sat on a stool and studied the lockbox. It looked harmless enough: just a brass box with a knob on one side. Of course, she didn't know what bad magic would look like. What she did know was that this box had worked once before, with no ill effects. She breathed deeply, then looked at Rufus.

"Where shall we go first?"

She knew where she should go first: she should go to the passageway where Arkwright had attacked her father and his men. They must have been close to the wizard's lair, or he wouldn't have risked it. But Celie wasn't ready to take that on yet. What if he caught her and put her to sleep? How long would it take for someone to find her?

"Let's start with Mummy and Daddy's room, shall we?" Celie said to Rufus.

Rufus sneezed, and Celie took that as agreement.

In her parents' bedchamber was a secret passageway that led to a tunnel that ended at the moat. The underwater passage also went back under the Castle, but it was too narrow to swim up for very long. Celie hurried across the main hall to her parents' room, heart pounding as she waited for Bran to catch her and ask what she was doing.

But she didn't see Bran, and no one else spoke to her. She ducked into her parents' room and locked the door with a sigh of relief.

Rufus prowled the room, sniffing at the rug where his own parents liked to sleep when they weren't holding court in the stable. But Celie went straight to the fireplace and opened the secret passage, putting her hand on the carved bit of the mantel that was really a cleverly hidden latch. A section of the hearth swung open, revealing a tunnel that smelled faintly of moat water.

Celie used a lamp to look down the tunnel, but couldn't see any sign of Arkwright. She closed the door and put the lock on top of it, turning the knob with a flourish as Rufus looked over her shoulder.

Nothing happened.

"Work! You have to work!"

She turned the knob again. She moved the lockbox so that it was directly over the little hidden latch of the trapdoor. Still nothing.

"What am I doing wrong?"

There was a telltale tingle in her brain, and the trapdoor opened. Celie was crouched so close to it that she nearly fell in. She managed to check her fall, but then she tucked the lockbox into the front of her gown and lowered herself into the tunnel. Rufus screeched and crowded in behind her.

"Rufus," she hissed. "You can't follow me!"

But he did anyway. And it turned out that he could follow her. Rufus was large enough for her to ride, but he was lean and could slink like a cat when he wanted to, which he presently did. As Celie looked back over her shoulder, she saw him fold his wings tight to his body and bend his legs so that he was creeping along behind her without even touching the walls of the tunnel.

"All right." She sighed.

As they crawled deeper, the smell of moat increased, and so did the dampness of the tunnel. Finally they were at the underground stream that ran out to the tunnel. Celie looked around, not sure what the Castle wanted her to do. Lock the grate between the stream and the moat? But then the water from the stream would build up and flood the Castle!

Rufus, who enjoyed baths greatly, had plunged right into the stream and was splashing around. His happy cries echoed, and the faint light glimmered on the roof of the tunnel. Celie looked up, noticing for the first time that the ceiling of the tunnel was smoothly fitted stone, like the rest of the Castle.

"This was made by the Builder," she said with surprise.

This tunnel, and the stream, had been part of the original Castle. Could she only use the lockbox on the things the Arkish had added? Or maybe the Castle didn't want her to get rid of the original tunnels and hidden passages. Master Humphries had told her that running out of water and food was the number one reason why a castle under siege had to surrender.

Had the Builder of the Castle included an underground well or stream to make sure that this never happened? It seemed very likely.

"All right," Celie said. "I won't close this tunnel."

She turned to start back up the tunnel, chirping to call Rufus. But Rufus ignored her. He was paddling upstream, away from her, and farther into the narrow darkness.

"Rufus, no!"

He kept swimming.

Groaning, Celie waded into the icy stream after him. The last time she'd tried to swim up the tunnel, she'd been barely eight years old, much smaller than she was now. Her feet had left the ground, and she'd had to start swimming instead of wading much sooner.

But as the tunnel narrowed, the water grew deeper, and at last she had to swim. Her head bumped into the ceiling, and the space between the top of the water and the roof was only about as high as Celie's head. This didn't seem to bother Rufus in the slightest. He was paddling along, still making happy cries, his head brushing against the ceiling.

"Rufus," Celie said a minute later, "we have to go back now."

Water was lapping at her mouth, and her head was pressed against the ceiling. Rufus didn't know how to swim, not really, and he certainly didn't know how to swim backward. It was too narrow for him to turn around, and deep enough that she couldn't feel the bottom, even when she held her breath and dived down.

"Rufus!"

Rufus surged in the water, and there was a dull thud. A hollow sound, like he'd hit his head on something wooden.

"Is there a door?" Celie gasped. She was having trouble keeping herself afloat. Her skirts were so waterlogged that she had to flail constantly to keep them from dragging her down.

Rufus screeched, and then he sank. Celie screamed, but Rufus must have just pushed off from the bottom. He came up out of the water with a leap and bashed into the trapdoor, flinging it open. He grabbed the edge of the door in his front talons and pulled himself through.

When Celie tried to climb up after him, she didn't have the strength. She was barely able to tread water and hold the edges of the trapdoor. Her skirts felt like they were weighted with lead.

Rufus leaned down to see why she wasn't following, and she grabbed frantically at the harness strap that ran across his chest. She tried to tell him to back up, but she choked on a mouthful of water instead.

It didn't matter, though, because Rufus got the message and pulled her out of the water, backing slowly away from the trapdoor. Celie was bruised and scraped by the time she'd made it all the way out, and was gasping and coughing on the stone floor beside the trapdoor, but at least she was alive.

"You're a good boy, my precious boy," she wheezed.

When she'd recovered enough, she looked around. They were in a narrow passage—an Arkish passage, she was sure—lit by a lamp on a small ledge. Celie closed the trapdoor and looked at it. It was identical to the one from her room, so she fished the wet lockbox out of her bodice.

"I hope this works. I don't know if it's not supposed to get wet," she said to Rufus, who was busy shaking out his wings, soaking her all over again.

When she put the lockbox over the latch, she could feel that it was going to work. She turned the knob and it locked onto the wood. Then she turned it again, and the door came loose from the stone floor. Another turn and the lockbox was free. Celie stuck it back in her bodice and staggered to her feet, gripping the wooden door.

"So that's how it works," Wizard Arkwright said.

The shadows peeled back from the wall and revealed Arkwright standing there, close enough to touch Celie.

Chapter
15

Celie screamed and ran.

She shouted for Rufus to follow her, and prayed that he wouldn't stay to fight. But Rufus must have sensed her fear, because she soon heard him on her heels, his talons scraping the floor as they fled Arkwright. Celie didn't stop to check if Arkwright followed, she just ran, her ears straining only for the sound of Rufus, not for anyone coming after him.

The passageway ended at a wooden door. Celie skidded through it, slamming it behind Rufus and nearly catching his tail. She put the lockbox over the latch and twisted the knob so hard, she nearly sprained her wrist.

The door fell against her as it came free from the blank stone wall. There was a *whoosh*, and the tingle in the back of her head flared like a sudden headache. The tingling shot down her back and into her arms and legs before ending suddenly at her fingertips and toes.

Celie staggered back and nearly fell before she managed to prop the door against another wall. She stood there and shook for a while, wondering what had just happened. The trapdoor in her room hadn't caused such a stir. Rufus looked distinctly ruffled, and was standing with his legs braced, waiting for the next upheaval. When it didn't come, he shook himself and began to preen.

Celie also shook herself, then ran her hands over the new wall she'd just made, checking for cracks, but the stones were as tightly fitted as the day they'd been built.

"Ha!" Celie said loudly, scaring Rufus, who squawked.

Arkwright was now sealed in that tunnel. If there was no other way out, he'd have to go through the water the way she had. Of course, that would lead him to the trapdoor that led to her parents' bedchamber . ...

"We have to find a way out of here," she told Rufus. "We have to warn Mummy and Da—and Bran. And the others!"

She turned and looked around, taking the lockbox off the door as she did so. They were in a small round room, and the only way out appeared to be up a spiraling flight of steps.

"Where on earth are we?"

Rufus sneezed—he didn't seem to recognize the place, either. So they went up the stairs, and up and up. There were no windows, and Celie was panting from the climb and the musty air when they reached the top.

"Another hatching tower?" Celie asked the question even though she knew the answer.

This wasn't a hatching tower. It was larger, and didn't have the sloping floor and enormous windows with sills that were shaped like perches. If anything, it was more like the Spyglass Tower where Celie and Lilah had once hidden from the awful Prince Khelsh.

There were no spyglasses here, though. Instead, each of the four windows had a different brass instrument mounted in it. One looked like some kind of strange compass, while another looked like a combination of a compass and a clock. There was a squat brass trumpet on the north side, and on the south was a tool that looked just like the one Bran used to chart the movements of the stars.

Celie gave the instruments a brief looking over and studied the view outside the four windows. This tower was on the opposite side of the Castle from the Spyglass Tower, so mostly what she could see was rooftops or the forested slope of the valley on the west side of the Castle.

Once she'd done that, she went back down the stairs, looking for another way out. Halfway down the long stone spiral, she stopped and grabbed for the iron handrail nailed into the wall as the Castle made a shift. When she reached the bottom, she found a door right beside the loose door she'd "unlocked."

"Huh," she said to Rufus. "I guess the Castle wanted us to see that."

He carked in reply. Celie struggled with the loose door and managed to carry it through the working door and out into a wide corridor that led past the guest rooms. She looked around, hopeful, but there was no one in sight who could help her, so she called Rufus over and made him stand still while she balanced it across his back. He looked like a very unusual seesaw.

"Just a little farther, boy," Celie coaxed him, holding the door on his back as best she could. "Just a little farther, and I'm sure we'll find someone."

But before they could find anyone, the door to one of the rooms swung open, knocking into the door Rufus carried and sending it flying. The accompanying twist told Celie that it wasn't a draft that had blown the door open, but the Castle.

Rufus, meanwhile, was sprawled across the floor gnawing on a corner of the loose door in anger. Celie picked up the door again and leaned it against the wall.

"Sorry, boy," she said to him. "I won't make you carry it again.

"Let's go see what the Castle wants, and then we'll find someone to help us carry the door."

The open door led to a guest room that looked just like most guest rooms in the Castle. It had a large four-poster bed, a writing desk, an armoire, and a scattering of chairs and ottomans—the usual odds and ends of furniture one found in the guest rooms. The tall, narrow windows were covered by heavy damask draperies.

Celie ran a hand over the desk and the chairs; she looked out the windows but couldn't see what the Castle wanted. She turned around to leave, but the Castle closed the door. She sighed and looked up at the ceiling.

"What? What am I looking for here?"

Rufus clacked his beak as though asking the same question, but the Castle didn't reply. Celie sighed again and reached for the latch of the door anyway. Her chin itched, and she scratched it against her shoulder as she tried to turn the iron latch.

The latch wouldn't turn, but it didn't matter. Celie had noticed something.

A panel of the dark wood commonly used in the Castle had been replaced by a lighter, honey-colored wood, which was smoothly polished but very plain. The wood paneling in the Castle usually had some sort of carving on it, even if it was just a band of angular leaf shapes at waist height. But this was as plain as—and the same width as—a door.

"Why, Rufus, I do believe we've found ourselves another passage," Celie said.

Rufus screeched.

Celie wondered why no one had noticed the different wood before. But this was the type of room used for distant cousins who only visited once a decade, cousins who usually wound up getting lost, turning left three times,

127

and jumping out a window. That was the only sure way to find the kitchens, where a kind maid (or often, Celie herself) would lead them where they were supposed to go. They would hardly notice or care that there were two kinds of wood lining the walls.

"Looks like we'd better lock this door, too," Celie said.

First, of course, she needed to open the door to see what was on the other side. She ran her fingers over the ridges of the wood, feeling for a tiny dent or hidden button that would trigger the latch. She probed back and forth, up and down, with careful fingers, and didn't find anything. Was she wrong? Was it really just a wooden panel that didn't match?

She put both hands on the wood, fingers splayed out, and started to run her hands downward, feeling for anything she might have missed before. There was a click and the door swung open.

"All righty then," Celie said, but her voice shook a little.

She peered carefully down the passage, but there was no sign of Arkwright or anyone else. Just a narrow corridor, dark and faintly musty. Celie took a cautious step forward, but Rufus pushed past her. He was on high alert: wings arched over his back, head twisting from side to side as he took it all in.

"Stay close to me," Celie whispered as she went all the way inside.

She closed the panel behind them and put the lockbox in the middle of it. She wasn't really sure where the latch was, but she hoped for the best. She had to hold the box up with one hand, since there was nothing for it to fasten to, and turn the knob with the other. But it worked, and the lockbox slipped into her hands a moment later. She felt the wall, and found that there was nothing but smooth stone now.

"Huh," she said to Rufus. "The door must have stayed on the other side. Oh, well, we'll just go get it later."

Then she turned around, and the realization struck her like a bolt of lightning. She felt her heart plummet to her shoes and stay there.

"What did I just do?" she whispered.

Chapter
16

She had no idea where this passageway led, or where the next door was. What if it was a dead end? Admittedly, none of the passageways that she knew of were dead ends. But there was always a first time.

"*Rawk*," Rufus said. His talons scraped on the stone as he started walking.

Celie fumbled the lockbox into her bodice and then hurried after him. She put out a hand and grabbed one of his wing tips, holding it just tightly enough so that she wouldn't lose him in the dark. Not that he could go far—the passageway was very narrow—but if it made any sudden turns, she wanted to be right behind him.

The passage made a sharp turn, and went on for a long way before turning again, but there was still no door to let them out. It was very dark, and Celie was starting to feel sick and panicky as they walked on and on. What if they never got out? What if she and Rufus were trapped in the walls of the Castle forever? Celie always knew which direction north was, or she had until now, and the realization that she didn't know which direction she was facing or where in the Castle she was made her feel like screaming.

Right before she gave in and started to scream or cry, she heard her mother's voice. A sharp tug on Rufus's wing pulled him up short. He carked softly, and Celie shushed him.

". . . certainly annoying," Queen Celina was saying. "But hardly a catastrophe."

"Our finest aged cheese!" Cook said indignantly.

"But no one was hurt," the queen said. "Or put to sleep."

There was silence, and then Ma'am Housekeeper spoke.

"Can the Royal Wizard not find a cure?"

"He's working on it," Queen Celina said. "I expect he'll find the counterspell any minute now. I'm helping as well as others."

"Oooh, I'd like to get my hands on that Arkwright," Ma'am Housekeeper said. "First he attacked my girl Maisy, then the king himself! And those poor guards!"

"And let us think it was the griffins, poor things," Cook added.

Celie's heart warmed. Dear Cook. She was a woman of few words and great skill with spatula and knife. She had accepted the griffins as a matter of course, though she refused to make them special treats, much as she refused to make special treats for Lulath's dogs, or indeed, any human diners.

There was another silence.

"Cook," the queen said finally. "There is something that I need you to help me with. We're going to need to keep the strength up for those who have been struck down. We'll need to feed them . . . something."

"Beef broth," Cook said immediately. "With red wine for the blood. And girls to feed them, one drop at a time."

"Yes, exactly," Queen Celina said.

"I have a pot on the fire now, Your Majesty. Just waiting."

"Excellent! Come with me, please."

Celie hadn't thought about that. The sleepers had no way of eating, and if they didn't eat, and starved to death while Bran tried to find a counterspell . . . she didn't *want* to think about it! Thank heavens her mother and Cook were taking care of matters.

But they were also leaving the room on the other side of the wall, heading to the kitchens.

"Mother! Mummy!" Celie called out. "Mummy?"

"I'm confident that we will find Arkwright very soon," Queen Celina said, her voice fading as she moved away from the wall. "In the meantime, I think I'll have guards posted in the kitchens. It's difficult to be clever when you're hungry."

"Mummy!" Celie shouted as loudly as she could.

There must be tiny holes in the rock, or cracks in the mortar, for her to hear them so clearly. Her mother had probably been checking on the plans for dinner when Cook had come to report that there was a cheese missing.

The talk of cheeses and starving Arkwright out of the walls made Celie's stomach growl loudly. She pounded on the wall with her fist and shouted for her mother again, with Rufus joining in, but to no avail.

They just couldn't hear her. Or if they did, they probably thought it was rats.

Celie thought again about the scratching in the walls, that day in her mother's solar when she'd been talking with Queen Celina and Lilah, and a chill swept through her. While she'd been sobbing over the new-found figurehead, Arkwright had been watching her, listening to her and her mother and sister. How many other private conversations had he eavesdropped on? Was she standing now where he'd been that day, and did her mother think she was just another rat in the walls?

Celie ran her hands over the wall but couldn't find any sign of a latch, or even a crack where she could pry her fingernails between the stones. There must have been some kind of spell that enabled her to hear what was happening but muffled the sound coming from her.

"This is probably how the Arkish spied on the Hathelockes, before they took over the Castle," Celie said to Rufus. "But that doesn't help *us*!"

She even took the lockbox out and ran it over the wall to see if it stuck to anything, but it didn't so much as twitch. She and Rufus moved on at last, reluctant to leave the soothing sound of the queen's voice, but desperate to get out of the passageway.

With a great deal of effort, Celie calmed herself and took hold of Rufus's wing again. She thought very carefully. Her best guess was that they were in the north wall of the queen's solar. And if that were true, then all she had to do was follow the wall past her parents' and Rolf's bedrooms to the corridor with the linen closets. That was where she and Pogue and the others had gone into the passages to find her father. This passage had to connect . . . if not to the linen cupboards, then to *something*. No one would bother to make a passage this long that had only one door. Not even an Arkish spy!

After a minute of walking, which still didn't lead her to any doors, Celie had to let go of Rufus's wing and push him along with her hands on his hindquarters. He didn't like the narrow passage or the darkness, and though he had been putting a brave face on it before, guarding Celie by walking ahead, she could feel tremors running through her dear griffin's muscles. They were moving at a snail's pace, which didn't much help Celie with her claustrophobic feeling.

"I know, darling, I know," Celie said. "It's dark, it's cold, we're hungry. But we'll get out of here soon."

Another turn and Celie felt a breeze. She put her hands to the wall and soon found a wooden door. With a wordless cry of triumph, she fumbled the latch open, but it was still dark. Celie put out a hand and felt fabric.

"It's a tapestry!" She almost screamed the words, she was so relieved.

She knew exactly where they were now. She thrust out an arm and flipped the tapestry out of the way, and she and Rufus stumbled into the corridor outside the winter dining hall, just a stone's throw from Rolf's bedchamber.

"Yes!" Celie yelled. "We did it!"

Rufus screamed as well, shaking himself and holding his wings out wide in relief. Celie quickly slammed the door and put the lockbox to it. The door came away from the wall so fast that Celie dropped it. It snagged the tapestry on its way down and ripped a long tear before hitting the floor with a crash. As the crash echoed through the corridor, Celie felt the twist in her head, and then an even stronger sensation that made her feel queasy. There was a grinding sound, like stones grating together, which brought two soldiers, a maid, and Bran running.

"Celie!" her brother cried, scooping her up in his arms.

"Oh, Bran!" Celie threw her arms around his neck and burst into tears, not caring who was watching.

"You foolish girl," he said. "You took the lockbox, didn't you? I've just ordered the guards to search!"

"It's all right, I'm all right," Celie said, trying not to sob as she spoke.

"Arkwright might have gotten you," he said severely, setting her down and giving her shoulders a gentle shake. "I can't believe you did this!"

"I just . . . we have to close the doors," Celie said.

"Your Highness, it does appear to be working," one of the soldiers said. He had set the door upright and was investigating the wall behind the tapestry. "There's no sign of a passageway here at all."

"Y-Your High Wizardness?" the little maid said in a shaking voice.

"Yes, dear, what is it?" Bran said gently, turning to her.

"What was that noise? It sounded like . . . like the time the princesses and the Crown Prince went away." She looked at Celie with big eyes.

"I heard it earlier as well," the soldier offered.

"It happens when I close a whole passageway," Celie said. "Well, that's what I'm guessing that sound is."

"You've closed an entire passageway?" Bran said in disbelief.

"Yes," Celie said with pride. "Two, in fact." She decided not to say that she'd seen Arkwright, and that he knew about the lockbox. "And this one"—she pointed to the blank wall—"actually had some spell on it. When I walked past Mummy's solar, I could hear Mummy and Ma'am Housekeeper and Cook talking, but they couldn't hear me. The Arkish must have used it to spy on the Hathelockes."

"I wonder if I could feel for it," Bran mused.

He moved to the wall, and the soldier stepped aside, holding the tapestry even higher so that the young wizard could put his hands on the bare stone. King Glower, with the crown and rings of the Builder of the Castle, could

136

probably have laid one hand on the wall and gotten a feel for things immediately, even though he was still learning how to use the magical tools that Celie and the others had brought back from Hatheland. Bran had only his own magic, but still, that was formidable. Bran had graduated from the College of Wizardry two years earlier than most student wizards, and was well respected by all who knew him.

Bran stood for a long time with his hands on the wall. Celie, the two guards, and the maid all held their breath and watched him. Rufus preened his feathers for a while, then got bored and lay down. After a minute, Celie quietly sat down next to him. It had been a very exciting day, and Celie wasn't sure how much longer she could remain upright.

"There's nothing there," Bran said finally.

"No, sir?"

The soldier holding the tapestry waited for Bran's signal and then lowered it back into place. It was hanging crooked now: a bit of the top had also torn, and the rip near the bottom gaped, showing the stone wall behind.

"I mean, there's *no* passage," Bran said in wonder. "Before, when I was walking through some of the passages with the guards, I could sense the passages around me, feel when a turn was coming. But there's nothing there." He looked down at Celie. "You've gotten rid of the entire passage," he said.

"No," Celie said. "Our mother has."

"Yes," her brother said. "I must—" He stopped, and glanced at the guards and the maid. Then he went on, regardless of their watching eyes. "I must apologize to Mother. This little invention of hers may be our salvation.

"Thank you for being brave enough to make use of it." Then he frowned. "But I still may ask Mother to punish you. If for nothing else, then for sneaking into my room!"

Celie yawned hugely, and the movement made her mouth water. "That's fine. Even though now there's one less place that Arkwright can hide. Well, two." She put one hand on her middle as her stomach growled. "Oh," she said, remembering. "Just keep an eye on the tunnel under Mummy and Daddy's room! I can't lock it, and now Arkwright knows about it."

"He does?" Bran said in horror. "How?"

"He saw me climbing out of the door after I'd swum up the stream," Celie said. "But I got rid of that door, too."

"He *saw* you? Cecelia!" Her brother lunged forward and took her hands. "Are you all right? Where on earth have you been today?"

"All over the Castle," Celie said, her stomach growling again. "But before you punish me, could I please have something to eat?"

Rufus screeched in agreement.

Chapter 17

When Celie woke up, she was so hungry she thought she might start chewing her own sheets. And they were her own sheets, though she didn't remember getting into them. Someone must have carried her to bed after she and Rufus had gotten some food. The last thing she remembered was drooping over a bowl of cauliflower soup in the Heart of the Castle while Bran gave orders to Sergeant Avery.

She hoped that her brother hadn't asked one of the guards to carry her. It was embarrassing enough that she'd fallen asleep right in front of them, without having to be carried like a child through the corridors of the Castle.

She sat up and looked around. There were cracks of light between her curtains; bright enough that she knew it was well into the day.

"I've missed breakfast and probably lunch," she deduced.

At the sound of her voice, Rufus stirred. He was draped

across the end of her bed, and he sat up and began to shake and scratch as he did every morning. This process, followed by a thorough grooming to make sure all his golden fur was smooth and every golden feather was in place, would take some time, so Celie got out of bed to get dressed. She was rather proud of the fact that she, a twelve-year-old girl, took less time to get ready in the morning than an animal.

As she went to her wardrobe, she saw a folded scrap of paper on the floor just inside her door. She picked it up and had to rub her eyes a few times before she was awake enough to make sense of it.

I have the lockbox. Yes, we will use it. No, you may not steal it and use it alone again. Get some rest.

Bran

"Get some rest?" Celie looked at the note in disbelief. "Get some rest indeed!"

Rufus stopped his grooming regimen to look at her, then went back to worrying at his hind claws with his beak, unconcerned with Celie's anger.

"Not a 'Thank you, Celie'?" she said to her closed door. "No, 'You did a good job'?" She crumpled the note and threw it on the floor. "No one even asking if I want to come along?"

Her voice was rising, but she didn't care. Who would hear her, anyway? They were all off using the lockbox themselves, as though she weren't capable of closing more passageways, just the way she had yesterday!

"I am so tired of being babied," Celie ranted. "I'm so

tired of all my discoveries being taken from me! I'm so tired of doing all the work, and getting none of the thanks!"

She shook her fist at her bedroom door, imagining her family all tiptoeing past her room like she was an infant taking a nap. Meanwhile they went about the business of hunting Arkwright and building the ship to put *her* figurehead on.

The door swung open.

Celie was in her nightgown, but she decided that if the Castle didn't want her to get dressed, she wasn't going to waste time doing so. She put on her slippers and grabbed a shawl from the foot of her bed.

"Come along, Rufus," Celie called. "You can finish grooming later."

Rufus leaped off the bed to follow with only a small squawk of protest.

The Castle was eerily quiet. It felt like the middle of the day, but there was no one around. Celie didn't know which way to go, so she went to the main hall. The front doors were open, as they always were, and there were two guards standing there. They both saluted when they saw Celie, and didn't appear to notice that she was in her nightgown. The golden light pouring in from outside told Celie that it was late afternoon.

Her stomach gave a painful growl. She was sure that even the guards heard it, and they were paces away. The Castle didn't indicate any other direction for Celie to go, so she went to find some food.

The kitchens were nearly deserted, which shocked her. Usually they were full of scullery maids and undercooks and the formidable presence of Cook herself. There was a pair of spit-boys turning a large roast over the central hearth, and two girls shaping dough for the small dinner loaves, but everyone else was gone.

"Oh, Your Highness!" One of the girls saw Celie standing in the doorway and wiped her hands on her apron, bobbing a curtsy as she did so. "What can we do for you?" She nudged the other girl, who turned, flustered, and curtsied.

"I—I just wanted something to eat," Celie said.

"Of course! What would you like, Your Highness?" The first girl bustled around, opening dishes and showing Celie berries, half a roast chicken, and some carrots. "I could make you a sandwich . . . ?"

"That would be fine," Celie said. "I'd like to just . . . take it with me."

She used to eat in the kitchens all the time, but hadn't done so in a while. Celie had spoken to this girl who was offering her food on several occasions, but she was embarrassed to realize that she couldn't think of her name now. There had been so much lately, so many adventures (which had turned out to be horrible, rather than exciting), that she hadn't visited the kitchens, or ridden her pony, or done any of the things that had once filled her days.

Rufus butted her in the back.

"Oh, and something for Rufus, please?" Celie said.

She rubbed his head fondly. She felt a little guilty admitting it, but Rufus was much more fun than a pony.

"Of course, Your Highness!"

The other kitchen maid stepped closer to Rufus, working up her courage. Celie nodded encouragement, and the girl held out her hand.

"My brother is a guard," she said softly. "He's put in his name to have a go at an egg."

"That's wonderful," Celie said.

"They're not half so scary, up close," the girl said, giggling a little as Rufus sniffed her hand. "Like a dog and a pony together."

"More or less," Celie said.

"What do you think your griffin would like to eat, Princess Cecelia?"

The first maid had quickly assembled a sandwich and some fruit on a tray, and was now looking around, a little confused. Ethan was the one in charge of the griffins' food, along with a team made up of stable hands and two under-assistants to the Master of the Hounds.

"Oh, hmm," Celie said. "I'll just have a look in the pantry."

Celie stepped into the big room, a shiver running through her. The room was always cold, even in the summer, and Celie was never sure if it was magic or just good engineering. She moved around the shelves, looking for something Rufus might like.

There was a scuffing noise, and an intake of breath from around the corner of the shelves.

"Hello?" Celie called. Apparently the kitchens weren't as empty as she'd thought. But whoever was in here certainly had been standing in the cold for a long time! "Do you need some help? Hello?"

Celie came around the corner of the shelves, and found herself face-to-face with Arkwright.

The wizard stared at her, his arms full of food. He had a cloak draped over one shoulder that looked like the noise-muffling cloak the Castle had once given her. She supposed that was how he'd snuck into the kitchens.

"I guess living on nothing but cheese isn't very pleasant," Celie said, recovering from her surprise before the wizard recovered from his. She gestured to the things in his arms. "Would you like a basket for that?"

Arkwright threw the food at her, whirled around, and ran. Celie ducked a flying armload of apples and shouted for help. The wizard ran out into the kitchens, tugging his cloak around him, and Celie followed. She ran past the gaping kitchen maids and the frozen spit-boys, following the equally silent Arkwright, whose cloak was indeed of the type that muffled every sound.

"Come, Rufus," she cried as she passed him, and her griffin followed.

They tracked Arkwright out into the hall, where he leaped into a cupboard and slammed the door shut. Celie yanked it open again, and pushed the shelves back to duck into the passageway right behind Arkwright. This was the same one they'd gone through the night they'd found her father tied up with his men.

"Why didn't they lock this door?" Celie panted, following the bobbing light of Arkwright's lantern. He was freakishly tall, and could run very fast for someone who was over five hundred years old.

Rufus surged past her, pushing her against the wall, and pounced on Arkwright, bringing the wizard down. His lamp flew out of his hands and smashed against the wall. The oil splattered and burned, and Rufus screeched and jumped back, but he didn't release the wizard's robes from his talons.

"The egg!" Arkwright cried in sudden anguish.

"What egg?"

There was nothing in the passage but the three of them, and the broken and burning lamp.

"There!" The wizard pointed at a turn in the passage-way just ahead.

The fire was between Celie and the turning. She climbed over Arkwright's legs and threw her shawl over the flames, hoping to smother them. She edged past and around the corner, feeling her way carefully in the darkness, and barked her shins on something.

Groping with her hands, she found an egg in a nest of blankets. It was extremely hot and rocked in excitement at her touch.

"You're about to hatch, aren't you?" Celie said to the egg, her words coming out too fast, too shrill. "That's why he wanted more food!"

It rocked again at the sound of her voice, nearly standing up on one of its narrower ends.

"It's mine!" Arkwright screamed. "My egg! Mine, girl!"

Rufus screeched and Arkwright cursed.

"Keep him down, Rufus," Celie yelled.

She had to get the egg out of here. When had he taken it? All the eggs were watched and accounted for, or they had been as of yesterday, anyway. This was probably the orphaned egg from the west hatching tower, the one that Rolf was hoping to bond with.

"Stay, Rufus," Celie shouted. "Don't let him follow me!"

Celie wrapped a blanket around the egg to keep its shell from burning her hands, and picked it up as best she could. It was too big for her to put her arms all the way around, but she didn't have far to go.

No one knew the Castle as well as Celie. In the past few days she'd been in several hidden passages that she'd never seen before, ones that ran through the newer parts of the Castle. But this wasn't the newer part of the Castle, this was the part that had always been in Sleyne, and now that she wasn't worried about her father or tripping over the tied-up guards, Celie knew precisely where to go.

She went straight for six paces and took the left-hand branch when the passageway forked. Twelve more paces and the backs of her hands smacked into a wooden door. She pushed through into a confusion of hanging clothes and shoved her way out of her brother Bran's wardrobe.

Chapter 18

She managed to stagger over to the bed and lay the egg down before she dropped it.

Celie could only pray that Rufus could hold Arkwright until she brought help. She ran out of Bran's bedchamber and into his workroom. She decided to see if she could brace the door to the wardrobe closed with a chair to buy more time, and grabbed the chair at his worktable.

But something caught her eye, and she froze. It was an open-sided box with a knob on top. Inside were some gears and a clear glass tube full of blue liquid.

"Bran is making his own lockbox!"

This made her even angrier than his note had, and she forgot all about finding something to wedge the door closed. How could he make their mother feel like she was wrong for "dabbling" in magic . . . then use their mother's creation to make his own lockbox?

But she didn't have time to dwell on it; she had to find help for the egg, and for Rufus. She headed for the door and nearly lost her balance when the Castle twisted her around again, and she found herself facing Bran's worktable.

"What?"

She turned around, and the Castle swirled around her again.

The only thing on the worktable that Celie even dared to touch was the lockbox. As soon as she picked it up, the Castle turned her around so that she was facing the door. She hurried out into the corridor, and found herself facing a narrow, curving set of stairs. She had no desire to make the Castle turn her around again, so she went up the stairs without protest.

At the top of the stairs was a tower room, the same tower she'd found earlier, with the odd tools mounted in the windows. Celie paused, not sure what to do. She didn't know what any of these were for or how they were supposed to help her summon someone.

She went to the trumpet thing, hoping that it would show her Bran or her mother or father, but looking through it revealed nothing.

"Wait," she said aloud. "It's a *trumpet*."

She sucked in a breath.

"Halloooo?" Her voice echoed across the roofs of the Castle. "Hallo!" she cried out with more confidence now: it was some sort of magic speaking tube. "This is Celie! If you can hear me: Rufus is holding Arkwright in the passage that leads from the linen cupboards to Bran's rooms. And there is a griffin egg on Bran's bed that is trying to hatch!"

That done, Celie started back down the stairs, but a griffin screamed right behind her. The noise scared her, and she caught herself before she could tumble headlong down the stone steps. Whipping around, she saw Lord Griffin swooping into the tower, carefully tucking his legs up to get past the speaking tube she'd just been shouting through.

"There's an egg about to hatch in Bran's room," Celie told him. "Bran's room."

He lowered one wing, inviting her to get on his back.

"I have to help Rufus," she told him. She was never sure how much the king of the griffins understood. "Ru-fus."

Lord Griffin stepped forward, lowering his shoulder to encourage her to get on. It would certainly come in handy to ride a very large adult griffin into battle with Arkwright, Celie decided, and climbed on.

The griffin swooped out of the tower and flew in a tight arc that brought him down in the main courtyard. He loped up the stairs to the Castle doors, where the guards saluted him and Celie as they started to pass, but then Lord Griffin stopped.

"Hurry," Celie said, "this way!" She pointed.

"Is something amiss, Your Highness?" The guard hesitated, and then he said, "We heard you. You sounded like a voice from heaven."

The other guard nodded fervently.

"Can we do aught to help?"

"Yes," Celie said. "Follow me!"

She led them through the hall, feeling a little strange to be sitting on a griffin as they walked along beside her. But Lord Griffin was a fast walker, and too tall for her to easily dismount. Besides which, he was headed right where they needed to go: Bran's rooms.

They burst into Bran's workroom and then his bedchamber, where they all froze in shock. The griffin egg had hatched, and a plump, moist baby griffin was rolling around on the bed in sticky bits of shell, cheeping happily. The maid from the kitchen, the one who had let Rufus sniff her hand, was feeding the little griffin pieces of a sandwich from a tray she held on her knees.

"Cora!" The guard on Celie's left leaped forward. "What have you done?"

The maid, Cora, leaped off the bed. "He was hungry, and no one was around," she said, defensive.

But the little griffin cried out, and she sat back down, cuddling him and feeding him more food. She looked at Celie with tear-filled eyes.

"I'm sorry, Your Highness," she said. "He was so hungry!"

"I know," Celie said. "They always are."

"And I know I can't keep him, but could I at least come and visit him sometimes?" the girl pleaded. "Or maybe my brother could have him?" She pointed with her chin at the guard on Celie's left.

Celie shook her head, and the girl let out a gasp of pain, her eyes clouding up.

"Oh, no!" Celie said, holding up both hands. "I didn't mean . . . I wasn't shaking my head because . . . I was shaking my head because you *can* keep him! He won't go to anyone else now! He's yours!"

"He is?" Cora looked down at the griffin with an expression of wonder and guilt mingled.

"If he's eating out of your hand, that means he's bonded to you. Forever," Celie explained.

Cora's expression of guilt deepened. "I'm so sorry," she said in a shaking voice. "I didn't know!" She looked at her brother. "I'm not on the list . . . I'm only a kitchen maid . . . what will the king do?"

"Nothing," Celie assured her. "Anyone could put their names on the list! That was only to tell us what people were interested in having a griffin. And the griffins don't care if you signed up or not. If one likes you, he likes you—it's not like they can read!"

"Really?" Cora's face was alight, and she put one arm softly around the little beast. "I can really keep him?" she whispered.

"You really can!" Celie said, and smiled at the girl.

Secretly, though, Celie was thinking that this would be another blow for Rolf. She did not want to be the one who told him that he'd lost another chance to bond with a griffin. It was becoming more than a little strange that the heir to Castle Glower didn't have a griffin, and Rolf had been jealous when Lilah had bonded with Juliet . . . Hearing that a kitchen maid had bonded a griffin by accident would drive him wild.

"We have to help Rufus," Celie said, drawing her thoughts back to the present and her own griffin. "Do you know where the griffin stables are?"

Cora nodded.

"Take your little fellow to the griffin stables. Ask for Ethan. He'll make sure you have everything you need," Celie said. She knew, too, that it would be rather a pang for Ethan, but it just couldn't be helped.

"All right," the girl said, in a daze. She looked up at her brother. "I'm sorry I got one first," she said.

"It's all right, Cor," he said fondly. "Wait 'til Mum and Da hear! They'll be so proud of you!" He reached out and tentatively patted the griffin's head. "What will you call him?"

"I'm going to call him Geoffrey, after Granddad," Cora said after a pause.

"That's a lovely name," Celie said, edging Lord Griffin toward the wardrobe. "But we *really* need to see to Rufus and Arkwright now!"

"Yes! Sorry, Your Highness!"

Cora clutched her protesting griffin to her chest and scuttled out while the two guards drew their swords and came in a line behind Celie. The grandeur of their group—the large griffin king, the princess, and her guards—was somewhat spoiled by the fact that first they had to fight their way through Bran's robes before entering the dark passageway.

One of the guards—Cora's brother—fumbled to a lamp and lit it. They made their way slowly along the passageway and around the corner, where they found . . . nothing. Celie let out a cry of anguish when she saw the empty passageway. Or not entirely empty: two golden-brown feathers lay on the stone floor. The other guard edged around Lord Griffin, picked up the feathers, and offered them to Celie with shaking fingers.

"We have to find him!" Celie said, taking the feathers and clutching them to her breast. "Right now!"

Lord Griffin surged forward, but Celie sat back, hard, and made him stop. She took the lockbox she'd been holding and handed it to the second guard.

"Take this back to the door we just came through," she instructed. "Put it over the latch, turn the knob, and the door will disappear."

"But, Your Highness," he said, eyes wide. "How will we get out?"

"There are two other doors along this passage," Celie said. "Locking Bran's door is one less way Arkwright can escape me. Us."

"All right, Your Highness," the man said. "I trust you."

"Thank you," Celie said. "Take that lamp and find us as soon as you're done."

She and Cora's brother, whose name turned out to be Trevor, started down the passageway. Lord Griffin sped up when they heard voices around the next turn, thinking it was Arkwright struggling with Rufus. But when they came around the corner, they found themselves face-to-face with Bran and half a dozen guards.

"*Cecelia!*" Bran held a lamp in one hand, the original lockbox in the other. "What are you doing here? And with him?" He gestured to Lord Griffin.

"Arkwright has Rufus," Celie said. "Rufus was holding him, down there." She pointed down the passageway to where they'd found the feathers. "I went to get help, and when I came back, he was gone!"

"He didn't go down this way," Bran said. "They must be that way." He pointed down the only other branch to this passage. "We've closed the other doors; he's running out of places to hide!"

There was a faint stirring in the Castle.

"What was that?" Bran cocked his head to one side. "That felt like someone closing a door!"

"It was probably the other guard with me," Celie said.

"What? But how!" her brother spluttered.

How was answered by the other guard running up to them, flickering lamp in one hand and lockbox in the other. He stopped short and bowed, panting, when he saw the Royal Wizard.

"My Lord Wizard," he gasped. Then he turned to Celie. "It's gone, Your Highness! Just like you said! There's nothing there but a blank wall now!" He held out the lockbox to Celie, who took it.

"Celie! That is highly dangerous," her brother scolded. "More dangerous than this one, even!" He held up the one their mother had made. "I haven't tested that lockbox yet."

"The Castle wanted me to have it," Celie protested. "And you shouldn't have left it lying about if you didn't want people to use it!"

"Lying in my room on my workbench," Bran said. "Where I'd only just finished it! It might have killed him!"

"What?" The guard wiped his hands down his tunic, his face ashen.

Celie felt like her face was so hot, it was probably glowing in the light from the lamps. She couldn't believe that her brother was scolding her now—*now*—when Rufus was in trouble.

"It didn't kill him, Arkwright has Rufus, and you can yell at me later," Celie snapped, and turned Lord Griffin down the other branch of the passageway.

Chapter 19

They found nothing down that other branch, either. Bran closed the door himself, and then they all shuffled back the way Bran had come with his guards, going out through the linen cupboard. Bran locked that door, and when he did, there was a great grinding noise and a wave of queasiness that told Celie the entire passageway was now gone.

"What do we do?" Celie said, tears dripping down her face.

The guards were spreading down the corridor in either direction, looking in the tall cupboards with their weapons drawn.

"Where's the nearest secret passage?" Bran asked. "The kitchens?"

"There's none in there," Celie said. "Not that I know about, anyway." She wiped her face with her sleeve and reflexively stroked Lord Griffin's neck. It felt strange to be riding him all over the Castle this way, but he seemed to want her to, and it was very comforting. "Lulath's room!"

"There's one in Lulath's room?" Bran asked. "Is that how you spied on him during the time Khelsh took over?"

Celie urged Lord Griffin along the corridor. It was funny to think that she'd once hidden from Lulath, not sure if he was evil.

"No," she said, "the secret passage is on one side of his fireplace. The Castle created the spy hole I used; it's not part of these Arkish passages."

Lulath's rooms were the largest and most luxurious of the guest rooms, a sure sign of the Castle's favor. It was how Celie had known that Lulath didn't mean her family any harm.

The Grathian prince was on the floor of his sitting room with a platter of meats, hand-feeding his dogs and griffin. His manservant bowed them in with a look of surprise, but Lulath appeared delighted.

"It is our fine only wizard and our best Celie!" he caroled, scrambling to his feet in a tangle of velvet and lace. Then his welcoming smile faltered. "Is more being amiss? Shall I to be sitting beside our much-loved King Glower if you are not?"

"Arkwright has Rufus," Celie blurted out.

"This cannot be a thing!" Lulath said in shock.

"We have to go through your secret passage, and seal it behind us," Celie continued.

"At once!"

Lulath hustled his little dogs into their pillow-filled canopy bed and told them to stay. Then he grabbed a sword from a nearby rack and whistled for Lorcan, who immediately became tense and alert.

"Lulath . . . ," Bran began.

"Have no fears, brother of my Lilah! I am knowing which end from which," Lulath said, and strode toward the fireplace as he buckled on his sword.

The wooden wall panels on each side of the fireplace were elaborately carved with angular flower shapes, exactly like the flowers on the Arkish tapestries. Lulath poked one of the flowers with a long finger, and the hidden door swung open.

"There are being lamps," he said in a quiet voice. "But I am thinking the lamps you do have will be light for us. Too much of the light, and we are proclaiming to this bad wizard that we come for him!"

"Let's go," Celie said.

Lord Griffin needed no further urging. He headed into the dark passageway with Celie clinging to his back, walking at a quick, smooth pace. Celie had never thought she'd be as close to another griffin as she was to Rufus, but there was something so strong and reassuring about Lord Griffin. It was, in a way, like being with her father.

"Princess . . . I mean, my Lord Wizard?" The guard who had sealed the door into Bran's room whispered loudly down the line. "Do you want me to close this door? Permanently? With that thing?"

"Best not, actually," Bran said. "We need to leave ourselves one escape route, why not Lulath's room?"

"It will please me to be the place of refuge," Lulath whispered.

"Yes, sir," the guard said, and edged back until he was at the end of the line.

There were more whisperings as they all shuffled along the passageway. Bran kept trying to make Celie get behind him, but she ignored him. He was so busy hissing at her that he didn't hear the noise, but Celie did, and so did Lord Griffin.

They both froze, and Celie gripped the golden collar that Lord Griffin wore. She squeezed with her knees and Lord Griffin started forward, walking softly but swiftly.

"Celie," Bran said.

Celie held up one hand and shook it fiercely in warning. Bran instantly subsided. Everyone hushed, and crept forward. The sound was growing louder and louder. It was a scraping sound, and some thumps, and then . . .

"Stop it, you fool beast!"

Lord Griffin leaped around the corner at the sound of Arkwright's shout. The others rushed after him, and in the light of the lamps they saw Arkwright struggling with Rufus, who was tied with black cords. Celie's heart clenched to see her beloved griffin bound like that. He was scrambling to get away from Arkwright, who was cursing and trying to drag him along the passage.

Lord Griffin let out a scream of rage that almost shook the mortar from the stones around them. Arkwright whirled around and shouted something in Arkish, his hands making a throwing motion toward Celie.

Horrible sticky webby stuff attached itself to Celie's face and hands and dropped down over the griffin she was riding. Lord Griffin squalled as the webs touched him. Bran slipped around them before Celie could even cry out and began shouting a spell of his own. Black ropes flew at Arkwright, and then Bran whipped around and spoke three sharp words at Celie and Lord Griffin. The webs shriveled up and fell away, and Bran was facing Arkwright again and shouting another spell.

Arkwright had deflected the black ropes, and now he was chanting as he dragged Rufus away from them. Rufus was fighting him even more wildly, and Celie was appalled to see that there was a muzzle around his mouth, keeping him from squawking.

The passageway was too narrow for them to get around Bran and surround Arkwright, so Bran had to face him alone, flinging spells and edging closer to the older wizard and his captive. Lord Griffin was quivering with rage, screeching his battle cry, but there was nothing else he or Celie could do.

Bran hit Arkwright with another burst of magic, and the wizard fell against the wall. Lord Griffin grabbed the back of Bran's robes with a talon and pulled him out of the way, then leaped forward. Celie held tight to the collar as Lord Griffin went on the attack. He slashed and bit at Arkwright, who cowered, screaming.

Lord Griffin rolled his shoulder, and Celie found herself dumped on the floor beside Rufus. That suited her fine, and she hurried to drag Rufus farther down the passage and get the ropes off him. They were horrible and sticky, and they melted away when she pulled them off. They also took quite a bit of fur and feathers with them when she pulled, making both of them cry.

Once she'd freed him enough that he could run, Celie stopped pulling ropes off Rufus and tugged his harness to make him follow her. She went just a little way down the passage, and turned back to yell something to Bran. What she saw stopped her cold.

Arkwright was in the center of a huge swirling cloud of magic. It looked like dust, if dust had sparkles in it. But even with the sparkles, the dust looked . . . unwholesome. Dimly, beyond the chanting, gesturing Arkwright, through the rising cloud of dark magic, Celie could see Bran preparing a counterattack. She took a step toward them, one hand raised to ward off the dust.

"Celie! Run!" her brother shouted. "And take this!" He threw the lockbox, the original one that their mother had made, through the magic dust. Celie caught it. "You know what to do," he bellowed. "Go!"

Rufus was already tugging at the back of Celie's nightgown, anxious to be gone. She climbed onto his back, cradling the lockbox one-handed, and Rufus took off running down the passage.

Celie barely managed to stop him when they reached the next door, yanking on the harness so hard they skidded and he nearly fell on his rump. They plunged through the narrow door and came out in a corridor barely wider than one of the secret passages. It led to the laundries and sewing room, and eventually out a new door that was just across from the griffin stable at the back of the Castle.

Trembling, Celie put the lockbox on the door, and turned the knob. The door almost fell on her and Rufus, and Rufus had to dance out of the way. Then she urged him along the corridor, past the steam-filled laundry.

There was another door that connected to that passageway, and she wanted to close it immediately. It was near the Heart of the Castle, and Celie wanted to make sure that Arkwright didn't get anywhere near that room, or the once-broken Eye of the Castle that he had hidden for hundreds of years.

But when she got to the end of the corridor, all she found was a door she didn't recognize. And when she opened it, she saw a staircase leading up. Celie got off Rufus's back and sent him up the stairs, too scared to argue with the Castle, and followed right on his heels. At the top of the stairs, she found herself in that tower with the brass instruments once again.

"What am I supposed to do?" Celie wailed.

The only tool she knew how to use was the speaking tube. And what was there to say? They needed to guard the passageways that were left, and catch Arkwright if he came out, but she didn't know where most of the guards were. Were they already in the walls? Were they out working on the ship in the meadow?

The ship. Celie had read a book of sea voyages last year with Master Humphries. She went to the speaking tube and did the only thing she could think of:

"All hands on deck! All hands on deck!" she shouted. "Meet in the Heart of the Castle! All hands to the Heart of the Castle!"

Chapter
20

⟨─≋─⟩

Celie ran down the stairs from the tower with the brass
instruments, now with Rufus crowding her heels, and
when she came to the last step, the Castle changed. She
stepped out into the corridor just behind the throne room,
and found herself facing a tapestry depicting the Battle
of Bendeswe. She flipped up the edge, opened the door
behind it, and looked into the darkened passageway. She
couldn't see or hear anything, so she closed the door again
and used the lockbox to get rid of it.

There was a tight feeling in her chest as she did so:
now the only way out for Bran and Lulath and the guards
was through Lulath's room. She knew that was what Bran
had meant when he'd said that she knew what to do, but
it still scared her. It meant that Arkwright, if he overpow-
ered them, could also escape through Lulath's room.

Celie ran down the corridor and into the main hall. There was a stream of people coming in the front doors and heading for the Heart of the Castle. They stopped to look at her curiously as she stood there in her nightgown, but continued on into the Heart as Celie pointed to the doorway, still catching her breath. Then Pogue peeled off from the crowd and jogged over to her, ignoring her signal to continue into the Heart.

"Celie! That was you, wasn't it? What's happening?"

"Get some guards," she said to him. "Go to Lulath's rooms and guard the secret passage in the fireplace." Her throat constricted, and she had to cough to clear it. "Either Bran and Lulath will come out, or Arkwright will."

"What?" Pogue swore, started to say something, stopped, and then told her, "I'm on my way!"

He pointed to a few guards who were trickling in, pulling them out of the crowd. It was strange to see how quickly they responded: Pogue had once been known for his brawls with the village boys, usually over a pretty girl. But now he was a knight and a respected member of the court.

"Come with me," he ordered the men. "And you," he added, pointing to a young page. "Bring my weapons to Prince Lulath's rooms!"

He headed out with six men trotting behind him. Queen Celina came to the open archway of the Heart and looked out at the people still coming in. She saw

Celie and beckoned her forward. Celie hurried through the clusters of maids and confused ship workers to her mother, who put an arm around her and led her inside. Just before they stepped through the doors, Celie directed one of the maids to go to her room and fetch her copy of the Castle atlas.

Lilah was sitting close beside their father's cot at the front of the room, where the Eye of the Castle rested in the middle of the mantel. She was holding one of the king's hands, and looked as though she hadn't slept in days. Rolf stood guard on their father's other side, also looking exhausted and rumpled. Celie felt a little pang— she supposed she should have taken a turn sitting with King Glower. Then she shook it off. No, what she was doing was just as important.

Rolf's frown eased a little when he saw Celie, but instead of coming toward her, he pulled a bench out from the nearest table and gestured for Celie to stand on it.

"Tell us what's happening," he said when she got closer.

Celie took a moment to look down at King Glower. He appeared to be sleeping peacefully, if anyone could sleep peacefully in the middle of a crowded, well-lit room, fully clothed in the middle of the day. Celie stooped and kissed her father's cheek, then got up on the bench with Rolf's help.

She wished she'd gotten dressed, but there was no time now. And she couldn't help but feel a little proud that neither her mother nor her brother had questioned her about why she had summoned everyone. She faced the assembly, her fists clenched in the long sleeves of her nightgown.

There were maids and footmen arrayed in front of her, standing between the cots of the fallen guards. Cook and her kitchen staff were still in their aprons, and Cook held a large ladle in one hand like a sword. Ma'am Housekeeper and her chambermaids were grouped around the sleeping Maisy. Celie's tutor, Master Humphries, whom she had been avoiding for a week now, had his spectacles off and was rubbing his eyes. The men who had been working on the ship still had tools in their hands, as did the stable hands. The guards and courtiers and Councilors were all gathered in the middle. And they were all looking at Celie.

"Who among you knows where the secret passages are in the Castle?" Celie asked.

A few people raised their hands, mostly the maids, she noted. They looked timid, though, and a girl near the front called out.

"Not all of them, Your Highness. Just the ones near our quarters."

"And some of those have been closed permanently," Celie said, thinking fast. "All right . . . I'm going to break you into groups. I need you to guard each of the passageways while I try to close them. If Arkwright comes through the door you're guarding, stop him as best you can."

"Where is your brother?" Queen Celina said in a low voice.

"Wizard Bran, Prince Lulath, and a half dozen guards are in the passageway leading from Prince Lulath's rooms," Celie announced to the entire room, not trusting herself to look down at her mother as she said the words. "The king of the griffins is with them, and I have closed all the other doors from that passage." She looked at the atlas, which a maid had just handed her. "Does someone have a pencil I can mark this with?"

One of the Council leaped forward and handed her one he pulled from behind his ear. Celie began to cross out passages and secret door with heavy strokes.

Rolf held up a hand. "I want six men with me in the throne room," he called out. "The passage behind the dais." He pointed to Ma'am Housekeeper. "Ma'am Housekeeper, you take six men and two footmen to the other end of that passage.

"Celie?"

Celie nodded and marked the groups on the atlas so that they could keep track.

"Yes, Your Highness," Ma'am Housekeeper said. She snapped her fingers, and two footmen immediately went to her side. Sergeant Avery came to the front and detailed off six men for Rolf and six for the housekeeper, and they left.

"I'll take six men to the summer dining hall," the queen said.

"And two stout footmen," Sergeant Avery said. "To be your personal guard, Your Majesty."

Again he separated out some of his men and some of the servants, and they came to stand beside the queen. Celie made more notes, but her mother didn't leave. She looked up at Celie, waiting to see what was next.

"Lord Sefton?" Celie looked around for the tall Councilor. He had been one of their few allies during the dark time when Prince Khelsh had been in power. "Do you know about the passage by the Council's privy chamber?"

"No," he said. "I'm afraid I don't."

"I do, Your Highness," said one of the maids. "I clean the privy chamber."

"If you'd be willing to guide us, miss?" Lord Sefton said courteously as Sergeant Avery assigned more men to them.

"Of course, milord."

They left, and Celie assigned more maids and guards to see to the remaining passages. There were only three passages left now. Sergeant Avery would go to the stables with his last four men and three stable hands, Ethan would take more stable hands and a footman to the rear of the Castle, where there was a passage that had only recently arrived in Sleyne, and that left Celie and the weapons gallery.

Celie looked around in dismay. "I seem to have done a poor job of dividing up the guards," she said to Cook, who had drawn closer with her staff, not that everyone else had cleared out.

"Not really," Cook said, and she waved her ladle.

In the corners of the room were griffins, all the griffins that Celie had brought from Hatheland save for Lord and Lady Griffin and Lorcan. Juliet was on the alert beside Lilah, and Rufus was also watching Celie as though awaiting orders.

Cook, not one to be daunted by wizards or griffins, shouted to the beasts and brandished her ladle. The griffins immediately rose and paced forward until they stood in a cluster in front of Celie's bench, gently forcing the kitchen staff out of the way.

"Very well," Celie said to her golden-eyed army. "Thank you, Cook. You and your people may return to the kitchens."

"If you don't mind, Princess, we'll go back to guarding the stores," Cook said gruffly.

"What?" Celie stopped scribbling in the atlas and looked at the large woman. She remembered how empty the kitchens had been earlier, an eternity ago, when she'd found Arkwright in the pantry.

"I took my strongest people down to the storerooms this morning, to keep watch for that bad wizard," Cook said. "He's getting food from there, you know. Stands to reason there's a door none of us know about." She polished the bowl of the ladle on her sleeve in a way that made the huge spoon seem more terrifying than a sword.

"You'd best get back to guarding the storerooms, then," Celie said, blinking.

Cook nodded and snapped her fingers at the kitchen staff. They all filed out without a word.

Celie pointed to the griffins. "All of you! Follow me, please!"

She climbed onto Rufus's back and took the shortest route to the weapons gallery, which was filled with strange weapons and armor from the Glorious Arkower and Hatheland. At the head of the flock of griffins she went out of the Heart of the Castle, through the main hall, and into the clear space of the main courtyard. She turned Rufus and gave the order, and they all leaped into the sky and circled around the center roofs of the Castle until they came to the open gallery that ran along the west side.

They swooped down and into the long open-sided corridor that ran along the portrait gallery. Then through the portrait gallery, with pictures so ancient that Celie and her family now knew the oldest were of the Hathelocke and Arkish men and women who had come to Sleyne with their dying griffins. On the other side of that, across a narrow foyer, was the weapons gallery.

The door to the secret passage was in an alcove behind a suit of bronze armor, and led straight to the throne room. Before the Castle had been brought entirely to Sleyne, this door hadn't existed and the passageway behind the throne room had only appeared on Mondays, when the maids cleaned the throne room and the royal bedchamber.

171

"When this is done, I'll have to throw my atlas away and redraw every map," Celie grumbled to Rufus.

And it would be nice to know that no one could sneak through the Castle undetected. Her discovery that the Castle couldn't see inside the secret passages had made Celie feel like Arkwright was watching her all the time. She knew he was probably more concerned with her father or Bran, but still, it was a decidedly creepy feeling.

Again she realized that she was still in her nightgown. In her nightgown, and waiting for a wizard who meant her family harm to burst out of a secret passage. She looked around for a minute, thinking, and then she slid off Rufus's back.

"You all stay here," she told the griffins, pointing to the alcove with the suit of armor.

They stood rigid, watching, as though they knew exactly where the door was and had always known. Perhaps they had, Celie thought, as she slipped into the weapons gallery. She looked around until she found what she wanted: a leather jerkin with steel bosses down the front and back. It had probably been made for a young human prince, that or a dwarf warrior, but it was only slightly too large for Celie.

She hadn't been allowed in the weapons gallery until very recently. When it first appeared, it had thrown the Castle into an uproar. The first things anyone had touched had shot out bolts of lightning or, at the very least, stung the person's fingertips. Bran and Pogue had carefully gone over each item to figure out what its uses were and defused the ones that were dangerous.

Even then Bran had wanted to keep the weapons gallery closed, but King Glower had objected. He didn't like keeping secrets from his people, and it actually made the maids *more* nervous to think that there was a room they couldn't clean because it was too dangerous. So Bran had carefully given tours to all the staff, and then to his family and the Council, and no one had been injured. But he still checked every week to make sure that the weapons were in their proper places and not throwing off strange sparks or odors.

While Bran had been giving the family a tour, he had made the mistake of explaining to Rolf the lance that shot lightning. Bran had showed them all how it worked because Rolf wouldn't stop asking, and Bran seemed to think that, if Rolf ever *did* steal it, at least he'd know how to use it properly. Their mother had made Rolf swear a solemn oath not to ever touch the lance again, and Rolf had reluctantly done so.

But Celie hadn't.

There were actually four copper lances that shot lightning. Celie located the shortest, lightest one. It had a small pack that was worn on the back and connected to the lance with a coil of wiring. Celie pulled on the pack over her jerkin and picked up the lance in trembling fingers. She had put the lockbox on the pedestal where the lance had rested, so she hurried to adjust the tiny knobs on the side of the lance's grip that turned on the lightning power. The long copper rod began to hum and grew warm in her hands, and Celie carefully switched it to her left hand and took the lockbox in her right.

"Now I'm ready," she told the griffins when she came out of the gallery.

She straightened her shoulders, trying to settle the jerkin. The griffins sidled around her uneasily, sniffing at the jerkin and the lance. The younger griffins, including Rufus, didn't seem to like the lance very much, and couldn't calm themselves even after they'd inspected Celie and her weapon. But the older griffins went even stiffer, ignoring Celie as if she'd committed some terribly embarrassing faux pas. But now they faced the hidden panel with erect heads and half-raised wings, as though, even though they hated them, Celie's weapon and sort-of-armor made them take matters even more seriously.

"I'm guessing these are Arkish?" Celie said aloud, but none of the griffins looked at her.

They just watched the hidden door and waited.

Chapter
21

Λnd waited.

Celie didn't know what to do after a while. The griffins remained alert, but she slumped against Rufus with the tip of the lance resting on the floor in front of her. Her nose itched, but she didn't have a free hand to scratch it. She was desperate to know what had happened to Bran and Lulath, but she had no way of finding out.

No one had come to tell her to lock one of the doors, which could be good or bad. Perhaps Pogue and Bran had come, triumphant, out of the passage and into Lulath's rooms. Perhaps they were using the other lockbox to close the passages, working their way up to the gallery. Perhaps they were fighting with Arkwright somewhere, or just waiting him out, as she was. Celie didn't really know which of these options was better.

She had decided to fly Rufus to the main courtyard and get an update on the others, when the Castle gave a great heave. All the stones went an inch to the left and resettled, or so it seemed, and Celie nearly fell down.

But there was no accompanying twist in her brain.

"That wasn't the Castle," she whispered, her mouth dry.

Whatever had just changed had been Arkwright doing something *to* the Castle. Why had it never occurred to them before now: Arkwright might have made the secret passages! He had been there when his people had taken over the Castle, had tried to have griffins of their own, and failed. In retaliation they had created the plague and killed their own people.

"Or maybe it was Bran?" Celie said to Rufus, who was staring down the corridor, his entire body aquiver. "Bran could change something, couldn't he?"

But even though Celie loved and admired Bran, she had to admit that he wasn't a powerful enough wizard to do something that would alter the Castle against its will. No wizard alive was . . . except for Arkwright.

"Come on, Rufus," Celie said. "Let's go down to the courtyard and find out what's happening."

Rufus wouldn't move. He was staring down the corridor. All the griffins were.

"What is it?"

There was a wooden panel on the wall at the end of the corridor. Because it was carved with pictures of people and trees, Celie had always thought of it as being part of the portrait gallery. It was fixed to the wall with large copper rivets shaped like nine-pointed stars, or at least, it had been.

Now it had swung open as if it had hinges, becoming the door to a passage that hadn't been there five minutes before.

The griffins surged forward. Celie dropped the lance, dragging it behind her by the cord as she ran with them to the end of the corridor. One of the griffins peered into the darkness of the passageway beyond, then squawked and sat back on his haunches, looking at Celie expectantly. She tiptoed forward and looked inside. There was nothing as far as she could see. There wasn't even a shelf with a lamp to light the passageway.

"Hello?"

No answer.

Celie slammed the panel closed, put the lockbox in the middle of it, and turned the knob. The panel fell toward her, and she pushed it back against the wall. She scooped up the lance in her free hand and started to go back to the door they were supposed to be watching.

A groan as though the Castle itself was in pain tore at Celie's heart. There was a grinding sound and a quiver in the stones beneath Celie's feet. The griffins turned like hounds on the scent and raced into the portrait gallery.

"There!" Celie cried, pointing with the lance, but they had already seen it.

A portrait of a man with a high forehead and a nose like the prow of a ship had swung away from the wall. Celie checked inside again, but still saw nothing but a darkened passage. She slammed the portrait shut and locked it. It fell off the wall and she let it, not even caring that the frame smashed on the stone floor. She wanted the picture tossed on the dung heap when this was all done.

The grinding and groaning and shaking had started again. But this time, it went on and on without stopping. Celie urged the griffins forward like bloodhounds, searching for new passages. There was one in the weapons gallery, and another halfway down the stairs that led to the next floor. Celie locked and locked, letting the doors fall down in her wake—there wasn't time to set them back up again.

And still the Castle shook and groaned.

Celie's stomach was churning. This reminded her too much of the distressed Castle sending her to Hatheland a few months before. She couldn't bear to go back there, not alone! After the fourth door, she found that she was having trouble seeing because she was crying without noticing it.

She wiped her eyes on her sleeve and continued on.

After working her way down two flights of stairs to the winter dining hall, she ran into Pogue.

"Celie!" He gripped her shoulders. "Are you all right?"

"There are too many doors," she said in a daze. "I keep closing them and closing them!"

"Good girl," Pogue said, his face grim. "But have you seen Arrow?"

"What? No?" Celie looked around at her griffins, though, just to make sure. "I don't have him. I thought you had him!"

"I think he's . . . I think Arkwright took him. And Lady Griffin. And Lorcan."

"No," Celie said, and she nearly collapsed, slumping in Pogue's hands. "He can't have . . ."

"He came through Lulath's room. It was like a dust storm . . . I couldn't see anything! When my eyes cleared, he was gone and so was Lorcan. Bran and the guards were right on his heels, and they ran out of the room before I could even ask what had happened. But Bran turned around and threw me this as he left."

Pogue let go of Celie and pulled the half-finished lockbox out of his tunic.

"I locked that door, and I've locked the others I've found," Pogue said. "But I can't find Bran or Arkwright, and there's at least three griffins missing!"

"Go," Celie said. "Find them. I'll close more doors."

"Are they all done upstairs?"

"Yes . . . no!" Celie felt the bottom drop out of her stomach. She never had locked the door she'd been guarding. The one that had been there all along. "There's one left. I'll take care of it. Find the griffins!"

"Right!"

He turned and ran in one direction and Celie went in another with her flock of griffins. Back up the stairs, down the corridor, another flight of stairs, and then along the gallery.

Celie drew up, panting, in front of the suit of armor and the wooden panel. But it looked just the same: shut tight and untouched. The shaking and groaning had stopped, and in the stillness all Celie could hear was her own ragged breathing.

And then it happened. Too quickly.

Chapter
22

The panel slid open, and Arkwright was there.

Celie's eyes were nearly closed as she caught her breath, and she'd lowered the lance, which weighed heavy in her hand. The tip of the lance was stuck in a crack between two of the floor stones. She jerked upright and tried to heave the lance into position. It grated unpleasantly on the stone and made Arkwright hiss at her, stopping in his tracks. The griffins hissed back, and Celie tried to shout, but it came out as a sort of croak.

"Are you all that's left?" Arkwright looked like he might laugh. "Are you all that's stopping me? A little girl and her . . . pets?"

It was always a shock to see how tall he was. Celie wondered for a brief, stunned moment why no one at the College of Wizardry had ever questioned that he might be from another world. Really, he was frighteningly tall, with too much forehead and too little eye. He loomed over her now, smirking.

"Nothing amusing to say? No threats?"

"S-s-surrender," Celie said. She was squeezing the handle of the lance, but nothing was happening.

"Surrender to *you*? Why on earth would I do that? You don't even know how to hold a shockwand, let alone use it!"

That was when Rufus attacked. Celie wasn't sure if it was because Arkwright threatened her or because of what Arkwright had done to the griffin earlier, but either way Rufus simply snapped. Screaming his battle cry, he leaped at Arkwright.

"No, Rufus!" Celie cried out, remembering what had happened last time.

But last time, Rufus hadn't been surrounded by other griffins, also ready and eager to fight. Also, Arkwright clearly hadn't expected Rufus to attack him.

Six griffins went after Arkwright. Six griffins, clawing and screaming and biting. All Celie could do was stare for a moment, feeling like she was in the middle of some terrible dream and couldn't wake up.

Arkwright was screaming, but in the middle of his screaming, he lashed out with his long hand and a whip of fire slashed across Rufus's face.

Rufus wailed with pain and Celie rushed forward, pushing between the griffins. She brought up the lance, trying to jab Arkwright with it and make him back off. The lance exploded, lightning shooting out of the end, freezing them all in their tracks as the lightning struck Arkwright full in the chest.

The wizard made a gargling noise and collapsed.

Celie threw down the lance and the power pack and screamed. She didn't know what else to do. She'd killed him! She screamed and screamed while the griffins squawked and circled around her and Arkwright, sniffing at them both and snagging the hem of her nightgown with their talons.

"Celie! Celie! Stop it!"

Bran was in front of her, shaking her to make her stop screaming, but she couldn't. Finally he put one hand over her mouth and wrapped his other arm around her in a crushing hug.

"You're all right," he whispered forcefully into her ear.

Celie stopped. Then she started to sob. "But I k-k-killed him!"

"No, you didn't," Pogue said. He was kneeling beside Arkwright. "He's just stunned, Celie," he assured her. "More's the pity," he muttered.

"The pity?" Celie's voice broke.

"Pogue!" Bran snapped. "She's upset enough!"

"I'm sorry, I'm sorry," Pogue said. "I'm sorry, Celie . . . I just . . . I shouldn't have said that."

"I *didn't* kill him?"

183

"You just put him in a deep sleep," Bran said soothingly. "The shockwands aren't lethal. And besides, it's very hard to kill a wizard."

"Though he tried hard enough with you, Bran," Pogue said darkly.

That made Celie settle down, so that she could take a good look at her brother. His clothes were scorched black in places, and he had a gash along one cheek and a burn blistering his left ear.

"Should we lock the door?"

Celie's voice cracked and she sounded a little wild to her own ears, but she couldn't look at Arkwright and she didn't know what to do next. Had she and the griffins really defeated him? Was all this over?

"Good idea," Bran said.

Since he was closest, Pogue went to the door and called out, "All clear!"

They waited a moment, but there was no answer. He nodded to Celie, who came forward with trembling hands and used her mother's lockbox to seal the door. When she did, there was a grinding noise and a twist as the Castle erased the entire passage.

"Looks like Rolf did his job from the other end," Pogue said.

"But where have you *been*?" Celie wailed. "Did you find the other griffins?"

"The other griffins?" Bran looked around, counting feathered heads.

"I didn't have time to tell him," Pogue told Celie.

"Where's Lord and Lady Griffin?" Bran asked, then paused and stared at Pogue. "And Arrow?"

"Lord Griffin was with you! I haven't seen Lady all day," Celie said.

"You don't think Arkwright's locked them away somewhere?" Bran looked at Pogue and then counted the griffins again as though he couldn't believe some were missing.

"I don't know," Pogue said. "You take care of *him*." He kicked at Arkwright's leg. "Celie and I'll find *them*."

"Very well, but stop that," Bran said before Pogue could kick Arkwright again.

"Fine." Pogue reached out and stroked a few griffin heads, looking expectantly at Celie. "Well, where do we start?"

Celie blinked, her eyes sticky from crying. She picked up the shockwand's power pack and the lance and handed them to Bran; then she rubbed at her eyes and cheeks with the dirty cuff of her nightgown.

"I think," she said tremulously. "Oh! Rufus!" She turned to her darling. "Rufus? Find your father! Find him!"

Rufus turned in a circle and sniffed the air. He looked curiously at Celie, not sure what he was supposed to do. Celie pointed in one direction, then the other, asking him which way to Lord Griffin. He shook out his wings, looked at Arkwright, and hissed.

"Not much help there, eh?" Pogue rubbed his face with one hand, and caught his lip on the edge of the ring that

King Glower had given him when he'd been knighted. "Ouch! At least it wasn't that pointy-looking griffin ring of your—" He broke off and looked at Celie.

"We should ask the Castle," Celie said, coming to the same conclusion.

"Yes, just thought of that, too," Bran said. "Do you think it will answer, even if it's you and not Father?"

"Can't hurt to try," Pogue said, and he ripped the hem from his tunic and started to tie Arkwright's hands with it. "Give it a go, Celie, won't you?"

"All—all right."

Celie went to the wall and put both hands on it. Bran had tried to convince their father that he didn't need to do this, but he persisted. Celie had a sneaking suspicion that it made her father feel more at ease, because he didn't have to stand in the middle of the room while they all stared at him. It certainly helped her to focus her thoughts.

"We—we need to find the griffins," Celie said. "If you please. Lord and Lady Griffin, Lorcan the Destroyer—"

Bran let out a snort. They were all endlessly amused by Lulath's choice of name for his griffin.

"Arrow," Pogue said.

"And Bronze Arrow," Celie added.

There was a twist. A wall groaned. And an archway opened up just across from them. Through the archway, they could see shallow stone steps leading upward, and hear a sound of griffins squawking and crying—

186

"That's a baby griffin," Celie said, recognizing the sound instantly.

She forgot her exhaustion and worry and raced Rufus up the stairs. She could hear Pogue's heavier steps coming behind them, and started running through a list of what they'd need: food, people for the griffin to bond with, blankets—

But when she got to the top of the stairs, she found that they weren't needed after all.

The stairs led to a hatching tower, as Celie had guessed, and in that tower were gathered all the missing griffins, who hadn't been kidnapped at all. There was Arrow and Lorcan, Lord and Lady Griffin, and even Juliet. They were all squawking and flapping in excitement, hovering over the new baby griffin, which was held tightly in the arms of its new person.

Ethan.

Ethan cradled his little griffin in his lap, feeding it bits of bread. His face was shining with joy.

"She wants *me*," Ethan said, looking up at Celie and then Bran. "She does, I promise! I didn't have to trick her or force her; she came right to me!"

"Of course she did," Pogue said, and he went forward and clapped Ethan on the shoulder. "No one deserves a griffin more than you do!"

"I didn't know what else to do," Ethan said. "We went out to the stable, but the guards were so much better equipped than I was, and there was no sign of Arkwright.

So I came here to check on the egg. I know I wasn't supposed to leave my post, but then I thought, Arkwright might try to steal this egg; it was due to hatch any day now. So I came up here to guard it, and then they came." He gestured to the griffins that had been with him in the tower. "I thought they were just here to help me stand guard, but then it hatched."

"What will you name him?" Celie asked.

"Her," Ethan corrected her. "She's a she." He gazed down at the griffin lovingly. "I'm going to call her String of Pearls," he said, and stroked the feathers around her neck, which were marked with cream-colored spots that did indeed look like a necklace. "I'm afraid that's more the style of the original griffin riders than names like Rufus and Juliet," he said, sounding apologetic.

"Bran will certainly approve," Celie said.

Ethan's face fell. "But Crown Prince Rolf won't," he said in a hushed voice. "I know that the prince wants a griffin very badly."

"And you also know that you can't force them to bond with you," Celie said. "I'll tell Rolf myself. You'd better take String of Pearls down to the kitchens and get her more food."

Ethan scrambled to his feet, holding String of Pearls tightly in his arms. The griffins all batted at him gently with their wings, carking their pleasure at the pairing. Ethan headed down the stairs, a river of gold and brown and cream bodies following after him. Last of all was Lady Griffin, who took the stairs at a stately pace.

"Your mother feeds her far too much cake," Pogue said; then he froze.

"Your mother," he repeated. "Your *mother*. The *queen*."

"What's wrong?" Celie said in alarm, clutching his elbow. "What's happened?"

"Nothing," Pogue said, starting to move again. "But something terrible's going to happen when she finds out that you captured Arkwright and no one told her!"

Chapter 23

When she found out they'd caught Arkwright, Queen Celina was too happy to be angry. Or at least, to be angry for very long. And there was the excitement of the two new griffins that had hatched in the last day, and trying yet another counterspell on Arkwright's still-sleeping victims, and what to do with Arkwright himself now that he'd been captured.

And that last proved to be the real problem. What do you do with a wizard who's turned evil?

"You give him to the Wizards' Council," Bran said. "I sent for someone to remove him ages ago. He should be here any day now." He rubbed his face. "He *should* be here. We can't—aren't supposed to—do anything else but wait for him."

In the meantime, Bran put a sleeping spell on Arkwright before the stunning effect of the shockwand could wear off. He had to renew it twice by the time the two members of the Wizards' Council arrived, but no one cared.

Because when Bran was mixing the ingredients for the sleeping spell, he had a sudden burst of inspiration. After he put Arkwright to sleep, he put the same sleeping spell on King Glower, the guards who had been struck down, and little Maisy.

"Bran, do you know what you're doing?" Queen Celina asked anxiously.

"They're already asleep," Rolf pointed out. "You can't make someone be more asleep. Can you?"

"Hush," Bran told them.

He counted to ten, and then he used the counterspell on them.

King Glower snored once. So did one of the guards. Maisy rolled over and nearly fell off her cot. But they still couldn't wake them up. Queen Celina, who had been gripping her husband's hand tightly in both of her own, bowed her head and a tear slipped down her cheek.

"I know you'll keep trying, Bran," she said softly. "And so will I."

"I'm not done yet," Bran said with a touch of asperity.

Celie knew that it made him nervous to have people watch him do magic, but they couldn't help themselves. Lilah and Queen Celina rarely left the king's side. Ma'am Housekeeper and several of her girls had stopped by to check on Maisy, and of course Rolf and Lulath and Pogue had come to see Bran's attempt to wake the sleeping victims.

Now Bran closed his eyes for a moment and Celie could tell he was pretending that none of them were there. He opened his eyes and began again. He put the sleeping spell on King Glower, then Maisy, then the guards. Then he counted to ten and used the counterspell. King Glower was snoring in earnest now, and one of the guards muttered something and swiped at his cheek as though it itched.

"One more time," Bran murmured.

He put the sleeping spell on them. He put the counterspell on them.

Maisy blinked her eyes. She saw Ma'am Housekeeper standing over her and squeaked. She tried to sit up, flailed a bit, and had to be held firmly down on the cot by her mistress.

"I'm sorry, ma'am, I'm sorry," the girl said, her voice hoarse from not having spoken in a while. "I—wait—" She seemed to realize where she was, and who else was there. "What's happening?"

Ma'am Housekeeper bent her head to explain softly to the girl, but Celie didn't bother to move closer so she could hear. Her father, the king, was groaning and stirring on his own cot. He finally sat up with the help of Queen Celina, who was crying openly.

"Now, now, none of that," he croaked. "We must find this blackguard Arkwright; then we'll have time for tears!"

Celie tried to stand near Bran and act grown-up, but then Lilah threw her arms around their father, sobbing.

"Daddy," she blubbered. "Daddy!"

Celie gave in. She flung herself on the end of the cot, also crying, and barely noticed when Rolf and even Bran joined in. By the time they'd gotten themselves under control and everyone had wiped their eyes and noses and explained to the king and the guards and the chambermaid what had happened, they'd gathered an even larger audience.

"It seems we have come precisely on time," said a voice from the doorway.

"I told you that we would," said another voice.

They all looked up to find two strange wizards in traveling robes standing there, observing the room full of crying people with bright, inquisitive eyes.

"I see you finally deigned to come," Bran said stiffly. Then he ruined his disdainful expression by having to take out a handkerchief and blow his nose loudly.

"Interesting," said one of the wizards. "Are you ill, or are you moved by some type of emotion?" He took out a piece of paper and a pencil and waited to record Bran's response.

"This is being of the new," Lulath said in a low voice.

✦ ✦ ✦

And he was right: the two new wizards were as different from Arkwright as could be. Both were barely taller than Celie and as round as egg yolks, with long gray beards. They were so alike in their size and mannerisms that it would be easy to mistake them for brothers, except that one was as pale as a fish and the other dark-skinned. They were grave and kind and everything Celie had always thought a wizard would be, except for one small thing.

They wanted nothing to do with Arkwright.

"He has hidden himself in plain sight of the Council for hundreds of years," Wizard Roland said. He was the pale one. "This indicates a level of magical power that none of us can contemplate."

"It may not be just his skill, but the type of magic he practices," argued Wizard Bowen, his brown counterpart. "Or it might be both."

"Precisely," Wizard Roland said.

"That isn't precise at all," King Glower said, impatient. They were all anxious to be rid of Arkwright, and the air in the throne room was tense. It was two days after they'd arrived, and they were still refusing to even look at the Arkish wizard. "Unless you mean that's precisely why you should take him away immediately! The man is a menace! He's made his plot to take over Sleyne very clear. He attacked me and several of my men, and he nearly destroyed the Castle! I want him out of here!"

"But you are in the pink of health now," Wizard Bowen said. "And the Castle is none the worse for wear. The Castle has contained him. We cannot."

"How can you be sure?" Celie blurted out. "You haven't tried!"

"Ah," Wizard Bowen said, looking her over. "The girl who loves the Castle."

"The girl the Castle loves," Wizard Roland corrected him. "An interesting specimen."

"I'm not a specimen," Celie said hotly. Beside her, Rufus made a rumbling noise that would have warned off someone more familiar with griffins.

"And the griffin," Wizard Roland said, marking the noise that Rufus made but not understanding what it meant. "Bonded. How strong of a bond?"

"My sister is not a specimen, as she said," Bran informed them. "I asked for the Council to send someone to help me contain Arkwright! If you won't do that . . ."

"Are you threatening us, Royal Wizard Bran?" Wizard Bowen just looked curious, and Celie wondered if they thought that Bran was also an interesting specimen.

Bran looked at them with his jaw clenched. "Do I need to?" He paced back and forth for a moment. "As the Royal Wizard of Sleyne, I'm authorized to take any measures I see fit to ensure the safety of the Castle, and the people therein. I tried to go through the proper channels, and I requested that a pair of wizards from the Council come to help me with Arkwright. It took you two weeks to make a three-day journey, and now that you're here, you're refusing to help!" Bran was pacing the floor again, snapping his robes out of his way with angry gestures.

"I don't have the luxury of waiting another two weeks for more members of the Council to decide if they'll come and if they'll actually help once they arrive," he continued. "And again, it shouldn't have to be said that my twelve-year-old sister—a princess of Sleyne—and her griffin are not research specimens!

"In short, gentlemen, if you will not remove Arkwright from the Castle today, I will be forced to rescind your invitation to the Castle." He stopped in front of them, glaring.

"Our methods are not always welcome," Wizard Roland said comfortably.

"We have been unwelcome guests in many houses," Wizard Bowen agreed.

"But those houses didn't spit you out the chimney when the invitation was revoked," Bran said coldly.

Celie tried very hard to continue looking like a princess of Sleyne and not cheer. It didn't help that Rolf was standing next to her and grinning widely.

"You did not seem so theatric or demanding when you spent a term studying with us," Wizard Bowen observed. "Is this the effect of your rank or the Castle itself?"

He took something out of his pocket and twisted it in his hands. It looked like one of the cloth measuring tapes that dressmakers used. He started toward Bran, as though eager to measure his height, then thought better of it and hid the tape away again. Celie didn't blame him; Bran's expression was forbidding, to say the least.

"He tried to destroy the Castle," King Glower said heavily. "He tried to kill me, and my wife, and my children. He tried to kidnap my daughter's griffin, to steal an egg on the verge of hatching. Bran has had to put him back to sleep twice already. He must be gone before he causes more mischief." King Glower thumped on the arm of his throne for emphasis. "We can send you with a full complement of guards to help watch over him," he added. "But he must be gone."

The two round wizards exchanged looks. Then they looked around the throne room, deep in thought. Then they exchanged looks again.

"Well?" Bran demanded.

His harsh voice startled Arrow and String of Pearls, who both squawked. The two strange wizards instantly focused on the griffins, then exchanged another look before Wizard Roland (who seemed to do most of the speaking for the both of them) spoke.

"We will take Arkwright, and deliver him to the College in Sleyne City," he announced. "But then you must let us return to study you all and the Castle and the griffins."

Celie's entire body went tense. They were going to come back and study the Castle and her family and their griffins? That sounded horrible.

"That is too broad," Wizard Bowen said, frowning, and Celie started to relax. "We will study the relationship between the Castle, the royal family, and their griffins," he corrected.

Celie felt herself go stiff with anxiety again. She looked to Bran, waiting for him to refuse, to tell these awful wizards to be on their way before the Castle tossed them out on their round bottoms, but Bran just stared at the wall behind the dais for a minute, then nodded.

"Fair enough," he said. "You will take Arkwright to the Grand Master, and when you return, you may study us."

Pleased, Wizards Roland and Bowen bustled off to collect their luggage and, presumably, Arkwright, while the court all stood and stared at Bran in stunned silence. Bran was looking at the wall again, but at long last he focused his eyes on King Glower, and then blinked around at the rest of the family and the court.

"What have you done?" King Glower said in a low voice, so that only those privileged to stand near the throne could hear.

"We need to get rid of Arkwright," Bran said, sounding strained. "And Bowen and Roland are the two best researchers on the Council. They aren't going to hurt anyone with their measurements and their questions, and at the end of it all, we might actually be able to understand why griffins bond with some people and not others, and how the Castle communicates."

There was silence, and then the king let his breath out in a whoosh.

"Very well," King Glower said. "That seems to be a fair trade, and I'm sure it wouldn't do any harm to learn more about the Castle."

"Who could possibly know more than we do?" Lilah said, looking dissatisfied. "We live here—we've even been to the Tomb of the Builder! Celie's the first person to actually map the Castle's rooms!" She rustled her skirts around. "I'm still mad that I sat there like an idiot, holding Father's hand during all the excitement," she muttered.

"You were being the safest," Lulath said, trying to soothe her. "And of a comfort to your father."

"Who was asleep and didn't even know I was there," Lilah said.

Celie looked at the tips of her slippers where they peeped out from under her gown and scowled. She appreciated the praise, but it also reminded her of how much work she had to do. Her atlas, which she had so proudly delivered to her family only a few months ago, and which the royal scribes had worked to copy and bind, were useless now. She'd been working to update them once the Castle had been made whole, but now she had to go back and remove the secret passageways.

"Do you know what I think?" Rolf asked, then continued before anyone could ask him what he thought. "I think it's going to be a lot easier to learn things about the Castle now. Arkwright admitted that he had destroyed any books written about the Castle. I think he must have put a spell on some of the old Royal Wizards, to keep them from studying the Castle too closely. I bet Roland and Bowen will be able to discover all sorts of new things, and when they write them down, their writing won't disappear!"

Now Celie felt even worse. What was she good for? Just to be studied by some odd ducks of wizards? Her atlas was outdated, and soon she wouldn't be the only person who knew the ins and outs of the Castle anymore.

"I'm going to see Pogue," she muttered.

She tried not to be curious about what her family would say after she left, and walked out of the throne room with as much dignity as she could muster. She nodded regally to the two guards who opened the doors for her, and the two who stood at the open doors of the main hall; then she hopped on Rufus's back and let him carry her up and over the outer wall to the sheep meadow.

Chapter
24

Tall stacks of carefully hewn wood were arranged under the roof. The figurehead had been brought out of the throne room, polished and oiled, and given pride of place at the front of the construction. Other tools that had been found in the storage room had been laid out on a table where they could also be cleaned and polished.

Celie guided Rufus down to land lightly on the turf just outside the big roofed structure.

Pogue stood nearby with the shipbuilder. Master Cathan, a famous Grathian sailor and shipwright, had arrived just the day before. They had another table, spread with plans, and were checking off lists of things that were ready to be loaded onto wagons. Celie felt a panicky flutter in her gut: her new wardrobe would be ready by the end of the week, and the ship probably would be as well, and then it was off to Grath!

"Of the wagons, we will have the need of ten," the shipbuilder was saying. It seemed that Lulath's odd way of speaking Sleynth was common to all Grathians, and not merely some quirk of the prince's.

"We can have as many as we need, of course," Pogue replied as Celie and Rufus approached the table. "And as many men as are needed to keep things secure. Guards, too."

"This is being, of the things I am doing this life, the strangest of them," the shipbuilder confessed, studying the plans again. "Ships are, in the usual, being built where the sea can be looked upon, not two countries from that sea!"

He picked up an old rusty tool that was at hand and used it as a paperweight for the lists. Glancing around, he saw Celie and quickly stood straight, then bowed.

"Your young Highness! To what is this the pleasure?"

Pogue looked up and smiled. "Oh, hey, Celie! Everything all right?"

The shipbuilder looked impressed at this casual greeting. Celie had heard that at first he hadn't wanted to work with Pogue, who was simultaneously a knight and a commoner, and whose actual place at court was as some sort of non-magical assistant to the Royal Wizard. But Pogue had quickly won the man over with his cleverness and his willingness to learn.

"I just wanted to see how it was going—" Celie began, but then she saw the tool the shipbuilder was using as a paperweight. "What is that?"

"Oh, what, this?" The shipbuilder picked it up and turned it around in his hands. "It is being called a . . . sextant, Your young Highness. It is being used for a thing to tell in which direction is the land the ship is sailing toward. But this one, which I hold, is being of no use. There is rust, too much, and a small piece that cannot be found."

"Obviously we'd like to use the one from the Castle," Pogue said. "But perhaps we could get one in Grath. We do want to have a few things from Grath on the ship, to show the combining of our two nations."

To his further credit, Pogue was able to talk about Lilah's impending marriage without grimacing now.

"If you wanted one from the Castle, I can get you another one," Celie said. "One that should work. Also, do you need a spyglass? And a barometer?"

"Ah, be not of the concern, Your young Highness," Master Cathan said courteously. "I am knowing, in my Grath, a very man of making such things."

Pogue gave her a little encouraging nod, though. "Are there some in the Castle already?"

"I can get them," Celie said.

"Please do," Pogue said. He turned to Cathan. "Let's at least have a look and see how they compare to the Grathian-made instruments."

Celie climbed back on Rufus, and had him fly up to the tower with all the instruments, the one that the Castle had shown her during her flight from Arkwright. The speaking tube had come in handy, it was true, but she was sure that it would be even handier to have on a ship.

Rufus swooped into the tower, and Celie slid off his back. She went to the sextant first, and it almost fell off the brass mount into her hand. She went to the other windows and took the compass, the barometer, and the speaking tube. All of them came away in her hand, a sure sign that the Castle wanted her to take them to Pogue and the shipbuilder. Celie made a basket out of her skirt, and carefully climbed onto Rufus.

Rufus either noticed the extra weight of the instruments or sensed that they needed to be careful, because he flew very steadily down to the sheep meadow. The weather was fine, and now some of the maids had brought out the Builder's sails and were spreading them out on the close-cropped grass. They were red and blue striped, like a circus tent, and when Celie got closer she could see that Master Cathan was staring at them with something akin to loathing in his eyes.

"Are they having of the holes so many?" he called to one of the maids.

The young woman straightened, and Celie saw that it was Pogue's oldest sister, Jane Marie, who was an expert at repairing antique tapestries. Jane Marie, always serene and kind, came over to the table just as Celie did. She bobbed a little curtsy to Celie and then turned to the shipbuilder.

"No, sir," she said. "Like most fabric that's been stored by the Castle, it's in perfect order. You wouldn't know that it's been boxed away for hundreds of years! It could have been put away last week."

"That's excellent," Celie said, spilling the instruments onto the table and then shaking out her skirt.

"Is it being so?" Master Cathan looked unconvinced. "This being a danger, when there is cloth of too great age. The threads that do make the seams also might have the weakening—"

"Actually, sir, it's all of a piece," Jane Marie said. "There are no seams and they aren't hemmed, either. They appear to have been woven exactly to size." She shook her head in amazement. "The loom must have been enormous. I wish I could have seen it," she said wistfully.

"My gown is made from fabric found in the Castle," Celie pointed out. "It looks like new, but was probably in the sewing room for five hundred years or so."

Master Cathan looked displeased, and gave Celie's gown a quick and almost offended look. "But will my only prince and his princess have nothing that will be of the Grathian making . . . ?"

"The furniture and decorative fittings will be Grathian," Pogue said. He sounded as though he'd said it a hundred times already.

"And here are these," Celie said, pointing to the instruments. "They're Hathelocke-made, I think."

Master Cathan turned them over in his hands. "These are being fine work," he had to admit. "Of a pity there is not a spyglass found. But in my Grath can such a one of fineness be made."

"We have *four* spyglasses," Celie said. "And they're magic. They show you whatever you want to see!"

Master Cathan looked uncomfortable at this. "Do they see . . . things that are usual?"

"Yes, I'll get one," Celie said.

Back on Rufus, and back up to the sky. She had not had a lot of time to go flying lately, which was a shame. Especially since she could fly in daylight now, and didn't have to hide what she was doing. Rufus clearly enjoyed it, as well, taking his time to weave around the hatching towers and swoop low over the central roofs before finding the open windows of the Spyglass Tower.

Arkwright was in the Spyglass Tower.

He was still asleep, laid out on the floor like . . . well, like a dead body. Except this dead body was snoring.

Celie looked around. No one else was here. She'd thought that Bowen and Roland would have left by now with Arkwright heavily guarded, but here he was. How had he gotten here?

Rufus squawked and nudged the wizard with one talon, but Arkwright didn't move. If he hadn't been snoring so loudly, Celie would have thought he was dead.

"Bran," she yelled. "Braaaaaan!"

She started to go down the stairs and call for her brother, but the Castle turned around her, and she found herself dizzily facing one of the windows. The spyglass mounted in that window slid out of its brass mounting, and Celie leaped forward to catch it before it could smash on the floor.

"Oh, okay," she said. "I'll take this first."

She made for the stairs again, but the Castle turned the tower, and she was facing another window. Holding on to Rufus's harness to steady herself, she looked around. Arkwright was behind her now, still snoring away, but Celie felt uneasy. She didn't like being here with the sleeping wizard. What if the spell wore off?

"Fine!"

She hurried to take another spyglass. The tower spun again. She took the third. The tower spun again. She took the fourth. When she had all four in her hands, the Castle seemed to settle, and she tried to go down the stairs, but there was no door.

She stuck two spyglasses in her sash, a third down her bodice, and switched the last one to her left hand so that she could climb on Rufus. Celie was terrified that the Castle would close the windows, too, but Rufus flew straight out the south-facing window without a problem. Celie urged him toward the courtyard so that they could find Bran, but there was a ripple that she could feel even in the air.

Rufus had to flap his wings frantically for a moment to stay aloft as a gust of wind nearly blew him into one of the hatching towers. When he had recovered and wheeled around, he let out a cry. So did Celie.

The Spyglass Tower was gone.

"Find Bran," Celie said in a shaking voice.

Chapter
25

Bran was in the courtyard when she landed. Everyone was. All gaping and pointing to the space above the Castle where the Spyglass Tower used to be. Everyone turned to stare at her as Rufus landed, and Celie immediately became defensive.

"I didn't make the Castle do that," she announced, pointing to the empty air.

"Thank goodness you're all right," Bran said, rushing over. "I don't know how he got free of my sleeping spell, and I can't believe I'm even saying these words, but Arkwright escaped."

"No, he didn't," Celie said. She pointed upward again. "I just saw him, still sound asleep, in the Spyglass Tower."

"The Spyglass Tower? But it's gone!" Bran said, stunned. "Where do you think . . . ?"

"I don't know," Celie said. "I went to get one spy-glass to show Master Cathan, and it made me take all four, and then it disappeared. The whole time that I was there, though, Arkwright was on the floor, asleep."

"This is highly unusual," said Wizard Roland, walking up.

"But very fascinating," Wizard Bowen said.

He turned to Celie and once again the measuring tape appeared.

"Oh, go on," she said, and held out her arms the way she would for the dressmaker.

He didn't waste any time. He started with the middle finger on her left hand and began to measure her finger, palm, wrist, and arm. He called out the measurements to Wizard Roland, who had taken out a small notebook and was writing down all the numbers. All the while Bran and Celie watched the space where the tower had been. After a few minutes, King Glower and Rolf came out, panting as though they'd run through the Castle.

"What happened?" King Glower said. Then, in almost the same breath, he said, "And what are they doing to Celie?"

"It's fine," Bran said, distracted.

He explained Celie's involvement in Arkwright's disappearance. King Glower began to splutter and Rolf started tossing questions at Celie one after the other, but Bran held up a hand.

"Do you feel it?" he whispered.

210

"I do," Celie said as Bowen measured her hair, first with the curls stretched out and then with them naturally coiled.

"Something's happening," King Glower said, standing very still.

The Castle was *humming*. As they all stood and watched, the Spyglass Tower reappeared.

Celie was on Rufus in a heartbeat.

Lulath came running out with Lorcan, and Bran yelled for him to follow Celie. Together they flew up to the Spyglass Tower and peered in the windows. Celie did not want to land beside the unconscious wizard again.

But he wasn't there.

Rufus hovered just outside the south window, and Lorcan went around to the north. He wasn't fully grown, and could only carry Lulath for very short flights, so he bobbed up and down a great deal, but even so, Lulath leaned over his griffin's wing and stared into the tower.

"For what do we look, our Celie?" he called.

"For Arkwright," she called back. "I don't see him. On the floor."

"No, there is only being the table," Lulath agreed. "My Lorcan must be going to return to the ground now."

"Yes, all right."

They flew back to the courtyard, where most of the court was gathered, pacing around and waving their arms. Bran grabbed hold of Rufus's harness before his feet even touched the ground.

"Well?"

"He's gone," Celie reported. "The Spyglass Tower is empty!"

"Are you sure?"

"Unless he was hiding in the chest," Celie said.

She'd meant to say it facetiously, but the worried thought came that he *could* have been hiding in the chest. But there was no way she was going to look. Bran or one of the other wizards could do that.

"I think he's gone," Rolf said. "I think the Castle got rid of him."

Pogue came running up with the Grathian shipbuilder on his heels. "Did the Castle just dump Arkwright in Hatheland?" Pogue asked.

"Is it doing such things with a commonness?" Cathan said, looking around nervously. "How is it to be known when it will not be liking you?"

"You're perfectly safe," Pogue said. "It wants this ship built."

"I think it did," King Glower said slowly. "I think it did take Arkwright to Hatheland." He had his hands pressed to each side of his crown. The rings, one like a griffin, the other shaped like a turret, glinted in the sun. "Arkwright is gone," he said in wonderment.

"Why?" Celie cried. She grabbed hold of her father's sleeve, then Bran's, wanting answers. "Why would it take him now? Why not before? Why not when we came home with the crown? Or before he escaped the first time?" She stamped her foot on the stones of the courtyard. "Why did you make us go through all this?" She waved her hand in a gesture that encompassed the entire Castle.

"Does it answer you often, when you speak to it this way?" Wizard Bowen held up a notebook, ready to write down Celie's reply.

"Now is hardly a good time—" King Glower said.

"Perhaps you aren't needed here after all," Bran said at the same time.

"Bran," Pogue said, interrupting them both.

"What is it?" Bran turned to their friend, impatient.

"The Castle wants Master Cathan here, to build the ship," he said.

"Yes, I know," Bran said, turning back to the other wizards.

"It hasn't gotten rid of Cathan," Pogue said.

"Of course it hasn't," Bran snapped. He pointed to Bowen. "If you want to study something—" He froze. "Oh."

"You don't think . . . ?" King Glower jerked his head at Wizard Roland, who was holding up the measuring tape and looked like he was just seconds from taking the king's measurements.

Pogue nodded. "Maybe the Castle wants us to know its secrets, now that it's all here, and you have the crown and rings, Your Majesty," he said.

"Oh," Bran said again. His face screwed up and he was thinking hard, looking from Wizard Roland to Wizard Bowen and back to the Castle.

"You think it waited to get rid of him until *they* came to the Castle?" Celie said. But she believed it; as soon as she spoke the words, she believed them. It just felt right.

"If Arkwright were gone, Bran wouldn't have sent for them," Pogue said.

"We wanted to come, but have had other, more pressing, duties," Wizard Roland said.

Rolf had an expression of dawning horror on his face. "You don't think the Castle let Arkwright loose to begin with, do you?" he asked in a whisper. "Just to bring them here."

"It would have been a cruel trick, but a necessary one," Wizard Bowen offered, scribbling away in his notebook.

"It's very like something the Castle would do," King Glower said. He sighed. "Fine, measure me," he told the hovering Wizard Roland. "We may as well do what it wants."

"It wanted the passages gone, too," Celie said, pressing a hand to her forehead as she thought it all out. "It wanted us to find the passages and get rid of them. Once Bran had called for help from the College, it could have locked Arkwright up in the kitchens, or any of the other places in the Castle that he went through. But it didn't."

"Devious," Rolf said, sounding admiring. "It got the Arkish passages removed, found two wizards to help crack its secrets, and once that happened, it finally got rid of Arkwright!" He clapped his hands. "That's our Castle!"

"It shows a more intricate intelligence than we have hypothesized," Wizard Roland noted. "It will be good to begin immediately, and not need to take Arkwright to the College and return."

Pogue gave King Glower a meaningful look. "Exactly what the Castle wanted," he said.

"No doubt," King Glower agreed, his arms still out-stretched. "Otherwise I'm sure we'd all be head down in the pig yard."

Queen Celina and Lilah, both wearing crisp new gowns that they had just received from the seamstresses, arrived in the courtyard.

"Now, what in heaven's name is going on?" Queen Celina asked. "And why is Celie carrying all those spy-glasses? She looks like a pirate!"

Chapter
26

It wasn't until a day later, after dinner in the summer dining hall, that Celie was able to propose her idea to her parents. Well, her parents, and Bran, Rolf, Lilah, Lulath, Pogue, Wizards Roland and Bowen, Master Cathan, and a handful of the Council who had been invited to the informal family dinner.

At least her parents would be less inclined to argue with her if there was an audience, Celie thought. And she'd had time to practice what she wanted to say in her room, and to get the feeling that it was what the Castle wanted her to say, as well.

"Father," Celie said. She felt even smaller than she had when she'd offered them all her bound atlases.

There had been a lull in the conversation when she'd spoken, and now all eyes were on her. She cleared her throat.

"I have an idea," she said.

"What is it, Celia-delia?"

Celie winced at the childish nickname but plowed ahead. "It's about the ship," she said, and she flicked her eyes to Master Cathan, who leaned forward a little around Lulath to see her.

"Yes?" he said, at the same time as her father made a gesture for her to go on.

"All these problems, with the Hathelockes and the Arkish, they've gone on and on for years, with the Castle in the middle of it," she began. "And we just got rid of the Arkish passages because we want the Castle to be Hathelocke, but also Sleynth because it's here now. But we still have the Arkish tapestries, and our family is part Arkish, and Ethan is Arkish, and that seems to be all right."

"Yes, that's true," her father said, looking confused. "Go on."

Celie drew in a deep breath. "We want the ship to combine things from the Castle, and from Sleyne, and also from Grath, to illustrate the connection between our countries, right?"

"Yes . . . ?"

Lulath briefly looked like he was going to toast her sentiment, but Lilah poked him and he subsided.

"But the Castle has parts of Hatheland and the Glorious Arkower in it, and I think the ship should, too," Celie went on.

"We are having and using of the pieces from here in this Castle, Your small Highness," Master Cathan told her. "You are bringing to us yourself, this very yersterday, the spyglasses."

"Yes," Celie said. "But I think those were Hathelocke-made. And so was the barometer. And the figurehead."

"What would you like to add, darling?" Queen Celina asked.

"The doors," Celie said. "Or at least use the wood, even if they're not still doors. The doors to the secret passages."

"I've already added the first trapdoor, from Celie's chamber, to the supplies," Pogue said, nodding his head at Celie as he clearly grasped what she was saying. "I don't know what kind of wood it is, but it's hard and strong."

"There are over a dozen," Celie said, nodding back. "Doors of all sizes. Some with beautiful carvings."

"We could be using of these things," Master Cathan agreed, but then a cloud passed over his face. "But not if they are being magic. Such magic has not a place on a ship of any country."

"If I may add reassurance, Your Majesty," Wizard Roland said. "We have, just today, inspected these very doors, which Wizard Bran keeps in his workroom. That is, I assume they are the doors the young princess is speaking of?"

Bran nodded. "They are."

"Excellent," Wizard Roland said. "Then you have probably also noticed that they have no magical properties?"

Everyone looked at Bran. Bran stared into space. "Well," he said. "There are none that I can find—"

"There are none," Wizard Bowen asserted. "The magic came from the Castle; the passages only had enough power of their own to remain in place, and not be closed by the Castle. Now that they are gone, their doors appear to be nothing more than doors." He made a sort of salute at Celie. "The princess has had a noble idea. With the addition of the doors to this ship, you will truly create something that represents all of Castle Glower, and all of Sleyne. And as it is built in Grath by a Grathian shipwright, then the Grathian element will also be added."

"What a lovely idea, Celie darling," Queen Celina said. "Truly!"

"If the wizards are all agreed that there is nothing magical about these doors, then I don't see why not," King Glower said.

Lilah stood up, walked around the table to Celie, and then put her arms around her little sister. She kissed Celie on the cheek.

"You amaze me," she whispered.

Celie felt herself turning bright red.

"To our only Celie," Lulath said, finally getting to raise his glass in a toast.

Celie had to stay standing while they toasted her, but then she sank down into her seat, still blushing. King Glower asked Master Cathan how long it would take for the ship to be readied to move to Grath, taking the attention off Celie, to her great relief. She felt strangely light.

Earlier that day she'd given the master copy of her atlas to Wizard Bowen, so that he could compare the old plan of the Castle with its new features. He'd promised to give it back to her soon, but Celie found that she didn't care. She wouldn't have time to finish it before they left for Grath, and she was sure that Roland and Bowen would do a much better job of mapping the Castle than she could.

"You really do amaze us all," Pogue said, leaning just slightly toward her so that he could talk in a low voice. "I could see it on your face when we sat down: you aren't happy about those two"—he indicated Roland and Bowen with a slight twitch of his finger—"finding out the Castle's secrets without you."

Celie didn't have to agree. She was too mortified, hoping that no one else had been able to read her expression as well as Pogue had. As they had sat down to dinner, the queen had asked the two visiting wizards how long they thought they would be studying the Castle, and Roland had shown not a glimmer of self-consciousness when he said that they might spend years unraveling the secrets of the Castle. Years that Celie would spend traveling to Grath and back again—who knew how many times!

"They might have measuring tapes and notebooks and magical training," Pogue went on, still speaking low enough that only Celie could hear, "but you understand the Castle better than anyone, and I have a feeling you always will."

Celie looked away, trying not to blush any more or start crying. She caught her mother's eye, and saw the queen nod slowly, approvingly. She had to find another place to rest her eyes, and took in the griffins lounging in the corners of the room. Her gaze sharpened, and the urge to blush or weep vanished.

Normally Lord and Lady Griffin held court near the fireplace, and the other griffins kept their distance, save for Rufus. But tonight, despite it being a very warm evening, they were lying on the hearth, as close to the small fire as they could get without singeing their fur. Added to that, there were half a dozen griffins in the summer dining hall, and all of them were very close to the griffin queen. Not even just close: Lord Griffin was curled around her, and the others were almost on top of Lady Griffin. Rufus had his head on his mother's haunch, and Lorcan was actually on her feet. Celie could hardly blame them; Lady Griffin's fur and feathers were like silk, and she'd continued to put on weight until she was as plump as a pillow.

As though sensing her interest, Arrow, who had been sitting behind Pogue's chair, got up and went to the hearth. He spread his wings and collapsed forward onto Lady Griffin, covering all but her head.

"What on earth . . . ?" Celie half rose from her chair.

"That's weird, right?" Pogue stood up. "I've never seen them do anything like that before." He whistled. "Arrow! Here!"

Arrow ignored him.

"What's the matter?" King Glower craned his neck to look over the high back of his chair. "Everything all right?"

Queen Celina, sitting at her husband's left hand, leaned back so that she could look at the griffins properly. She frowned.

"Celie," she said. "I really have been meaning to have you and Ethan look at my dear lady. Something is wrong with her, though she doesn't appear to be in any distress."

"She's more than a bit plump now," Celie agreed. "And she walks really slowly, but I think that's because she's overweight."

"Well, I think it's more than that. She sleeps all the time, and she never flies anymore," the queen said. "And I swear, I haven't been slipping her sweets, but she just gets bigger and bigger."

The whole pile of griffins wiggled around.

"Oh, good heavens," Lilah said. "They're practically *in* the fire. Juliet! Come away, love!"

Juliet paid no attention to her person. Arrow hadn't even looked up when Pogue had called to him, and Celie had a feeling that Rufus was watching her through slitted eyes. She guessed that if she called him, he wouldn't even twitch.

Celie turned to the maid who was just setting out plates of cake. It was Cora, who was herself the proud owner of a griffin.

"Oh, Cora," Celie said. "Where's your griffin?"

The girl turned pink. "Geoffrey? He's supposed to be in the griffin stables, Your Highness," she said.

"But . . . ?" Celie looked over at the fire. The only two griffins she didn't know were full-grown ones who had come to Sleyne with Lord and Lady Griffin, and they didn't have riders.

"He likes the big fire pit in the kitchens," Cora said in a rush. She turned her gaze to the king. "I'm ever so sorry, Your Majesty! I try to keep him away!"

"Heavens, child," the king said. "If Cook doesn't object, I can't see any reason why he can't be there. But has he been acting normally?"

"I think so, but he's only a week old," she explained. "And I've never seen a griffin up close before."

"Ah, well then," the king said. "Just eating and sleeping and more eating?"

"Yes, Your Majesty," the girl said with pride. "Geoffrey's a great one for eating."

"That's all right then," Celie said. "But could you run out to the griffin stables and ask for Ethan to come in? Thank you."

Cora set out the last plate of cake in front of Master Cathan, and went out with a curtsy.

"Does everyone but me have a griffin at this point?" Rolf said in despair.

Lord Griffin raised his head and made a sharp carking noise, as though shushing Rolf. Rolf put his head down next to his plate.

"It will be fine, darling," Queen Celina said. "You'll have one soon, I can just feel it!"

Wizard Roland whipped out a notebook and pencil. "Did this feeling just come upon you?"

"I beg your pardon?" Celie's mother looked startled.

"You are the magic user, the one with no training?" Wizard Roland flipped back through his notes to the front page and then nodded. "The queen? Your father was the Royal Wizard, yes?"

"Yes," Queen Celina said. Celie thought her mother looked a bit uncomfortable.

"You created the so-called 'lockboxes' that were used to seal the so-called 'secret passages,' yes?" He consulted another page. "Yes."

"Yes," Queen Celina said, looking ever more alarmed.

"My mother had my full permission and supervision," Bran said, looking pompous and wizardly to cover up the lie.

"Hmmm," Wizard Roland said, clearly not believing Bran's story.

"Someone possessing that level of magic should be at the College of Wizardry," Wizard Bowen said, but he sounded academic rather than condescending.

"Hmmm," Wizard Roland said again. "A queen has never attended the College, not in its four hundred and eighty-three year history," he noted.

"It would be too problematic for a queen to spend four years away from the seat of power of her nation," Wizard Bowen said. "Or a mother to leave her children for such a length of time is also unwise. Thus it has never been done."

"Which is unfortunate when one considers the fate of the queen's mother," Wizard Roland said.

Celie sucked in her breath, and Lilah uttered a small cry.

"Well," Queen Celina said, showing no sign of having taken offense. "Why don't *you* train me? You're going to be here for some time studying the Castle."

All three wizards—Bran, Bowen, and Roland—sat with their mouths agape. It had clearly never occurred to them.

"One must attend the College of Wizardry in order to learn magic," Roland finally said in a fussy voice.

"But I'm a queen and a mother, and I can't leave my family," Queen Celina countered.

"It's never been done," Bowen objected.

"Mother!" Bran said, sounding like he was about twelve. "What are you *saying?*"

"I'm saying, Bran, that it's time things changed," Queen Celina said. "There will be three wizards in the Castle for the foreseeable future. I need to learn magic so that I don't harm myself or those around me. Having you take turns privately tutoring me is the perfect solution."

"A very perfectness of a solution," Lulath said, clapping his hands. "Might I be having of lessons in magical weapons? They thrill me! And to my sadness, I have not the magic of the queen or our only Bran."

"What a lovely idea, Lulath," Queen Celina said.

Bran just sat there with his mouth open, aghast.

"You called for me, Your Majesties?" Ethan said, coming into the summer dining hall. He looked at the tense faces around the table. "What's happened?"

"I'm going to be studying to be a wizard, here at the Castle," Queen Celina said.

"Yes," Bran said, and remembered to close his mouth. He nodded his head slowly. "Yes, Roland, Bowen, and I will undertake to teach my mother. And, I suppose, show the others a few things."

Then Bran shook himself.

"But I'm sorry, that isn't why we called you here, Ethan," he continued. "We wanted you to have a look at these griffins."

"Ah," Ethan said. "Are you wondering when the queen will lay her egg?"

Chapter 27

I thought we were in an uproar when Arkwright was in the walls," Lilah grumbled. "Could this get any more ridiculous?"

Celie tried to answer, but the seamstress had pulled a velvet gown over her head, and she got a mouthful of fabric instead. When she emerged from the bodice, Lilah had carried on ranting, and Celie realized that she wasn't expected to say anything.

"Mother is studying to be a wizard, wizards are studying the Castle, Lady Griffin is going to lay an egg any day now, there's a ship to build even though no one from our family has ever been on a ship, and we're going to have to go to Grath by ourselves!"

"By ourselves? Isn't Lulath coming?" Celie managed to fit the words in before Lilah went on.

"Lulath doesn't count!"

"Then why are you marrying him?"

"Celie, you know what I mean!"

But Celie really didn't. Lilah was the one who always wanted things to be new and exciting: new clothes, new adventures, getting engaged at seventeen, traveling across the known world to meet his family; she was the one having fun . . . wasn't she? Celie was the one who didn't want to leave the Castle, or have things change.

And yet, now that there were wizards measuring and scribbling and mapping, Celie wasn't sure she wanted to be there to watch. Now that the pieces of the ship were ready to be taken to Grath, she was excited by the idea of the ship and the ocean. What did it feel like to ride atop the waves? What would the fabled isles of Larien look like?

"Are you listening to me?" Lilah demanded.

"Everyone in the Castle is listening to you," Queen Celina said, sweeping into the room. "They can't help it, Lilah! You really must not give yourself over to these hysterics!"

"*I am not hysterical!*" Lilah shouted. Then she turned red and said in a small voice, "I'm sorry, Mummy."

Queen Celina wrapped her arms around Lilah and held her older daughter in a tight embrace.

"Why am I scared?" Lilah said in a choked voice. "I love Lulath!"

"Getting married is scary," Queen Celina said. "It's a big decision, and it leads to even more big decisions."

"Is that supposed to help?" Lilah sobbed.

"Yes, darling, it is," the queen said. "It's supposed to help you remember that this isn't about gowns and going on holiday to the sea. It's about making choices, and thinking carefully about them before and after.

"And I want you to understand that your father and I wouldn't let you make this decision if we didn't feel you were ready for it, or if we thought you were making a terrible mistake. You will note that we did veto the idea of a spring wedding . . . unless the spring you're talking about is three years from now."

"I know, I know," Lilah said, pulling away from her mother and dabbing at her cheeks. "Yes," she said more seriously. "I do know. It's still . . . it's a lot."

Celie watched in silence as her mother hugged Lilah again, and thought how strange it was that she was usually the one having a hard time with changes, but now it was Lilah. Was this a sign that Celie was growing up? But that didn't make sense; Lilah was five years older than Celie, after all.

Queen Celina also seemed to come to this conclusion. Or rather, to think that Celie must be acting brave, when she secretly wanted to cry and scream, too. The queen let go of Lilah again and came over to hug Celie, who was now laced and buttoned into a stiff new gown.

"And Celie darling, I know, I know you hate to leave the Castle, but it's so wonderful that you'll be able to go with Lilah and help her! I know you'll be my brave girl!

And I'll be just a few weeks behind you, really. I only wanted to make sure I had a good handle on my magic before I joined you."

"That's fine," Celie said, "I'm not—"

Rufus burst into the room with a cry of triumph. He went straight to Celie and began to butt her with his head, pushing her toward the door he'd just come through.

"Rufus, where have you been? I've been looking for you all day," Celie scolded him.

Secretly she was relieved, however. She didn't really know what she'd been trying to say to her mother, because she didn't know how she felt.

"I haven't seen Juliet all day, either," Lilah said.

Rufus screeched and tried to shoo Lilah toward the door, too, flapping his wings. He was dancing from foot to foot, his talons making a horrible scraping noise on the stone floor.

"Something's wrong," Celie said.

"Is it Juliet? Where is she?"

Rufus turned and ran out, sure now that they would follow him. And they did: Celie, Lilah, Queen Celina, and one of the younger seamstresses who was told to go and see what the problem was.

The griffin led them through the lower level of the Castle, up the stairs, down the long corridor that ran between the throne room and the Heart of the Castle. As they came around the corner, Celie expected them to turn into the Heart, but Rufus turned the other way, down a small side corridor that led to Celie's parents' bedchamber.

"Oh, no! What's happened?" Queen Celina gasped.

"Juliet?" Lilah called.

But they went past the king and queen's rooms to the last door, the one that led to Rolf's bedchamber. The door was wide open, and Rufus plunged inside.

"Juliet?" Lilah called again as she, Celie, and Queen Celina all hurried after Rufus.

Juliet was in the room. So were Arrow, Lorcan, Lord Griffin, String of Pearls, and Geoffrey. Also Ethan, Pogue, King Glower, Cora the kitchen maid, Lulath, and Rolf. Rolf was standing beside his bed, his eyes wide.

"Do you think this means . . . that I . . . Is this one finally for me?" Rolf said, his voice rising to a squeak as he looked over at Celie.

Celie could only stare. The griffins and people were all huddled around Rolf's high bed. In the middle of the bed, in a nest of rucked-up blankets, was Lady Griffin. She was positively glowing as she curled around an enormous pumpkin-colored egg.

"Oh, she laid her egg," Celie said, and took a step forward, one hand reaching toward the egg to feel for the familiar silky heat.

Lady Griffin made a warning sound low in her throat, and Celie froze. Then the griffin mother turned to look at Rolf and made a humming noise, shifting so that her upper wing wasn't covering any of the egg, inviting Rolf to touch it.

Rolf reached out and carefully laid one hand on the egg.

"Oh," he said, and turned his face away to hide the tears welling up in his eyes.

"Joy! The very joy," Lulath exclaimed, and he began to applaud.

Lady Griffin screamed at him and he stopped abruptly.

"Perhaps we are leaving the beautiful mother to have the sleep," he said in one of his carrying whispers. "Come, my Lorcan."

They all began to file out, griffins and griffin riders, now that they had witnessed the laying of the egg that would be Rolf's. Rufus went forward to rub his head against his mother and father, who settled on the bed beside his mate to sleep. At last Rufus joined Celie, and they shuffled out of the room. Celie turned to look back as she closed the door, and saw her brother Rolf, the future king of Sleyne and Castle Glower, curl up beside the griffin egg with the king and queen of the griffins.

"Pogue," she said as the door shut on the scene. "Once we get to Grath, how quickly can we build the ship, and sail away?"

Acknowledgments

At the end of a new book I am always so grateful to everyone who made that book happen, and it makes me realize how many wonderful people help my books get from my brain to the hands of readers!

First and foremost, my amazing kids and husband, who are always there to cheer me on, and bring so much joy to my life. (Even if the kids do make finding writing time a bit of a challenge. Just a bit.) And of course a big hug and thank-you goes out to all my family, who have always, always been there for me and I know will always be there for me!

Love and gratitude to my agent, Amy Jameson, whose friendship has come to mean even more to me than her awesome agenting skills, and who seems to know exactly when to call me and give me a pep talk.

And thanks are long overdue for David Hohn, the gifted artist who has not only created the gorgeous covers for all my Castle Glower books, but also recently gave the Dragon Slippers trilogy a fantastic new look. I could not ask for better covers, David! Thank you again and again.

Thank you, too, to all at Bloomsbury, who continue to show their love and support for me and Celie and her Castle! Thanks and a big hug to my dear editor, Mary Kate Castellani, for being so good at spotting story trouble and so patient with my deadline-missing ways! Thanks to Cindy Loh, and to Lizzy Mason, Beth Eller, Linette Kim, Erica Barmash, Hali Baumstein, and Emily Ritter, who do so much for my books and who make working with Bloomsbury so much fun!

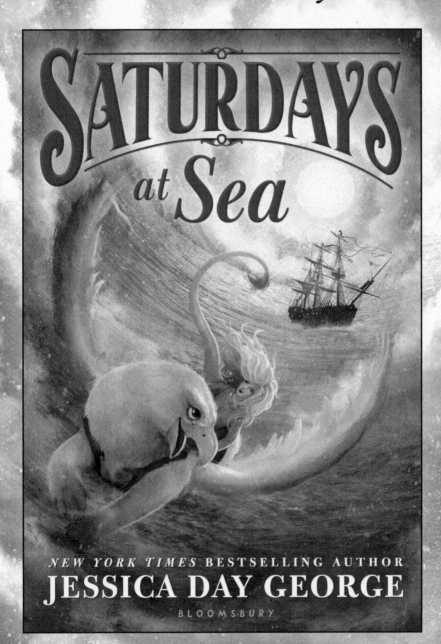

SATURDAYS
at Sea

NEW YORK TIMES BESTSELLING AUTHOR
JESSICA DAY GEORGE

Bloomsbury

This brilliant name is being all the thoughts of my Lilah," Lulath said later, as the two royal families, plus Pogue and various griffins and dogs, sat on the deck for breakfast. "As soon as it is being said to us, you two, you happy two, are having the naming of the ship, my Lilah is saying to me that it is being *The Golden Griffin!*"

They all raised glasses of fruit juice in Lilah's honor.

"It just seemed right," Lilah said demurely.

"Very much so," Queen Celina said. "I can't think of a more perfect name."

"I really thought it would be something about unicorns or puppies," Rolf admitted. "I've never been so glad to be wrong."

Lilah made a face at him.

"Well!" Orlath pushed himself back from the table. "Are we being ready?"

"Ready for what?" Celie asked.

She also got to her feet. She was ready for anything. Especially if it had to do with the Ship. Her heart started to pound.

"Is it time?" she asked Orlath. "Should we go?"

"Go where?" Queen Celina said, putting down her napkin.

"Anywhere," Celie said, holding out her arms. "It's a ship!"

"Anywhere in the harbor, correct?" Queen Celina said, looking from Celie to Lilah with a single eyebrow raised.

"Of course," Orlath said. "We must first test this magnificent Ship. We will take a simple cruise around the harbor to celebrate the betrothal and to test the soundness of the Ship!"

"A thing of great fineness," King Kurlath said, getting to his feet and reaching out a hand to his queen. "And a thing that you must all be enjoying your own selves."

"Oh, you are not going to sail with us?" Lilah said with disappointment.

"My our dear Lilah," Queen Amatopeia said. "It is being a very great secret that you must now be knowing." She looked around the table, very grave. They all stared back, suddenly silent.

"Here we are being a people of the sea," Queen Amatopeia said. "A people of the trading, and the ships." She shook her head sadly. "And my very Kurlath and I myself . . . we are being the sickest of seasicknesses. Were we to be going even unto this harbor, it would be this all the very time!" And then she made a highly indelicate vomiting sound.

Everyone stared at the elegant queen for a heartbeat. And then Rolf positively roared with laughter.

"Did you *really* just do that?" he demanded.

Queen Amatopeia looked pleased.

"Oh, my queen, you are being the most very!" King Kurlath laughed. "But"—he held up a cautionary finger—"she is also saying a truth. Even still do the insides of me go to and fro, as they went to and fro this yesterday at the river!" He shook his head. "Were they to go to and fro at this harbor, there would soon be to, and never fro!"

Rolf had to put his head down on the table. "That's the second best thing I've ever heard," he said in a muffled voice. He raised his head. "I'm going to use that some time, if I may, Your Majesty," he told the king. "If this coach hits one more pothole . . . I might to and not fro. . . . The perfect thing to say in such a situation!"

Now it was King Kurlath's turn to look pleased. He bowed to Rolf. "Be using it! Be using it with often times!"

"You really won't come?" Queen Celina asked, her brow furrowed.

But they insisted that they would not, and they took their leave with many hugs and kisses. They also gave orders to Orlath not to take too long, for although the betrothal celebration was now officially over, there was a family dinner that night, and possibly more dancing. If they were not too tired. This last was said in a tone that implied that the king could not imagine not wanting to dance all night, and Celie helped herself to another muffin as fortification against the day to come.

They saw the king and queen back across the gangplank to the dock, along with most of the servants. At Rolf's request they left breakfast there, in case he, like Celie, wanted more. But finally it was just the Glower family, Orlath, Lulath, and Pogue, along with the griffins and Lulath's girls. They all looked around in anticipation.

"And the now?" Orlath asked, flexing his fingers. "Are we being ready the now?"

"So the ready!" Lulath told him. "So the now!"

"Ready and waiting," Lilah said.

"Let's go!" Celie cheered.

The gangway was removed, and the ropes were cast off. Sailors ran back and forth on the deck, reeling in the ropes and getting the sails ready. Celie went to the helm to stand beside the huge wheel with Orlath. Pogue did, too, but the others went to the bow where they would have the best view.

Celie didn't care about the view. She wanted a chance to steer the Ship.

Orlath brought them about, as he called it, turning the Ship from the docks and letting it glide around the edge of the harbor. The wind was perfect, and so was the tide, he told them, and Pogue and Celie nodded obediently. Both of them had their hands behind their backs, trying not to clutch at the wheel themselves.

Orlath sensed this and continued to narrate everything he did. He showed them how the sails were brought down, and how the ropes were used to adjust them so that they caught the wind just right. He showed them how the turn of the great wheel moved the rudder so that the ship would go the direction you wanted.

As they approached the mouth of the harbor, Orlath turned to Celie.

"And now, Princess Celie?"

Celie didn't need to be asked twice. She grasped one of the handles sticking up from the wheel and held it just as she'd seen Orlath do. The wheel was warm and smooth under her hands, and it felt wonderful. She knew that Pogue was disappointed, and that he wanted to take a turn, but she didn't care. He could wait.

And then the wheel lurched to the side, and the boom swung to the side, shifting the main sail. The Ship began to leave the harbor mouth, rather than sailing past it and back around to the docks. Celie tried to turn the wheel, but it was too heavy.

"Ah, ah, ah!" Orlath said, laughing. "Not yet!" He took hold of the wheel on either side of Celie's hands and tried to turn it. It wouldn't budge. He grunted.

Pogue, seeing how Orlath was straining, also grabbed the wheel and tried to help them turn it, but still it would not move. The Ship began to sail out of the harbor with growing speed.

Several of the crew came forward, calling out to Orlath to find out if there had been a change of plans. He ordered them to reef the sails so that they would lose the wind and stop their progress, and they began to bustle about.

Lilah and Lulath hurried to the upper deck, concern written on both their faces.

"What are you doing?" Lilah asked, staring at the three of them trying to turn the wheel. "We're not supposed to leave the harbor!"

"Something's caught the rudder I think," Orlath grunted, speaking Grathian in his concern.

"Oh, no," Lilah said. "Is that bad? Is the Ship broken?"

"Oh, hardly," Orlath assured her. "We just have to get it into the dock and look."

There was sweat running down his face now as he tried to steer the Ship, but to no avail. There was sweat running down Pogue's and Celie's faces as well, and Celie's arms were shaking with the strain. It was like trying to move the Castle by pushing on one of the walls, and she said as much aloud.

"May I?" Lilah said.

She took over from Celie, and Lulath took over from his brother, standing shoulder to shoulder at the wheel of their Ship. The wheel didn't budge.

They heard a sailor swear, and looked to where the men were trying to get the sails down. But the ropes were whipping this way and that, slipping out of the men's hands as though taunting them.

"It's like trying to move the Castle," Celie repeated.

Pogue looked at her sharply. Rolf and Queen Celina had joined them now, and the queen appeared more thoughtful than concerned. Rolf just looked excited.

"Are we off to sea, then?" he said. "Excellent!"

"We're trying not to be," Lilah said from between gritted teeth. "There's something stuck on the rudder."

"Is there?" Queen Celina said. "Are you sure?"

"What is it, Mummy?" Celie asked.

"If you would be so kind as to tell the men to stop trying to reef the sails," Queen Celina instructed Orlath.

"Of course, madam," he said. He looked confused, but he called out the order anyway.

The men were also confused, but they let go of the ropes, which had continued to slip out of their fingers as soon as they were captured. Several of the men had climbed into the rigging, but now they dropped back down to the main deck.

The sails adjusted themselves. The ends of the ropes whipped around the belaying pins and tied themselves fast. The men shouted and prayed, and many of them fell to their knees.

"I think you can let go of the wheel now," Queen Celina said, looking rather grim.

"What's happening?" Orlath's voice was hushed.

"The Ship is taking us where it wants to go," Queen Celina said. "And I suppose we'd better let it."

Although Orlath was the captain of the Ship, which actually belonged to Lulath and Lilah, it was Queen Celina who took charge then. Well, the Ship had taken charge, but the queen took care of the people on board.

She ordered the food left from breakfast to be gathered up and stored properly, in case they needed it later. Then she had the cook check the other provisions that were on board and report back to her. They did, in fact, have enough food and water for a little over two weeks, he told Queen Celina, though he didn't look happy about it.

None of the crew did. They had rapidly left the harbor behind, and now they reluctantly unfurled the sails to find that the wind was in their favor. They were on the open sea, and though it was calm and the sun was shining, they didn't know where they were going, and they hadn't known that they would be leaving that day. No one had any spare clothes, and the crew's families were all expecting them home for dinner.

In the huddle around the helm they discussed ferrying the crew back to the docks on griffin-back, but it would take several trips, and most of the crew would not be too keen on riding a griffin. Not to mention the fact that if the Ship wanted to take them somewhere, they really should see where it was. The Castle had never done anything to hurt the Glower family, and Queen Celina told them that she had no doubt that the Ship felt the same way toward them.

"What do you think, Celie?" Lilah asked. "What do you think the Ship wants?"

"It's your Ship," Celie pointed out. "Maybe it's trying to make you happy."

Lilah blinked, and then her mouth dropped open. She looked from Celie to Lulath and then out at the open sea before them. She laid one hand on the wheel, and a smile slowly spread over her face.

"We're going to find the unicorns," Lilah whispered.

"Oh, good *heavens*," their mother said in despair. "Unicorns again!"

JESSICA DAY GEORGE

is the *New York Times* bestselling author of the Tuesdays at the Castle series, the Dragon Slippers series, and the Twelve Dancing Princesses series, as well as *Silver in the Blood* and *Sun and Moon, Ice and Snow*. Originally from Idaho, she studied at Brigham Young University and worked as a librarian and bookseller before turning to writing full-time. She now lives in Salt Lake City, Utah, with her husband and their three children. Her favorite day of the week is Friday because often there is pizza for dinner.

www.jessicadaygeorge.com

@JessDayGeorge

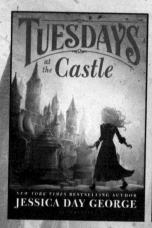

Don't miss the magic of fantasy and fairy tale from

Jessica Day George!

www.jessicadaygeorge.com